THAT STRANGER WITHIN ME

Shokooh Mirzadegi

That
Stranger
Within
Me

A Foreign Woman Caught
in the Iranian Revolution

Ibex Publishers
Bethesda, Maryland

THAT STRANGER WITHIN ME BY SHOKOOH MIRZADEGI
translation of *Bígáneh-yi dar man* from the Persian

Copyright © 2002 Shokooh Mirzadegi
Translation copyright © 2002 Esmail Nooriala

Manufactured in the United States of America

The paper used in this book meets the minimum requirements of the American National Standard for Information Services - Permanence of Paper for Printed Library Materials, ANSI Z39.48-1984

Ibex Publishers
Post Office Box 30087
Bethesda, Maryland 20824
Telephone: 301-718-8188
Facsimile: 301-907-8707
www.ibexpub.com

LIBRARY OF CONGRESS CATALOGING-IN-PUBLICATION INFORMATION

Mírzādah'gī, Shukūh.
[Bīgānah'ī dar man. English]
That Stranger within me : a foreign woman caught in the Iranian revolution / Shokooh Mirzadegi ; [translation, Esmail Nooriala].
p. cm. – (Modern Persian writers series ; 1)
ISBN 0-936347-83-x (alk. paper)
1. Iran—History—Revolution, 1979—Fiction.
I. Nooriala, Esmail. II. Title. III. Series.
PK6561.M555T4313 1998
891'.5533—dc21 2002   97-46022
                                        CIP

For Esmail Nooriala,
with all my respect and love

.1.

On Thursday August the ninth, 1979, at 3:30 in the afternoon, Amin's family, friends, and I became certain that he had definitely disappeared. Saeed, Abdol, and Ahmad had gone through all of the unidentified corpses in Tehran's central morgue and had told Nargess and me, waiting in the stuffy corridor filled with the repulsive smell of disinfectant, "He is not here."

I, Luba Lebi, a refugee from Czechoslovakia, was the daughter of Peter Lebi, who was a friend and comrade of Alexander Dubcek. I was an archaeologist trained in London and working as a curator for the Archeological Museum in Tehran. Amin Jalali, an Iranian doctor, was my husband.

Neither on that Thursday afternoon, nor for several months afterward, would I realize just how Amin's disappearance had intertwined my life with the Islamic Revolution in Iran.

While Saeed, Amin's cousin, was saying "He is not here," I was looking at Abdol, whose relieved expression revealed his naïveté; he did not realize that, despite our love for Amin, we had hoped to find him in the morgue. Had he been there, we would have at least known where he was.

Neither Abdol, nor the others, however, could know that the major cause of my own worries was my son, Bardia, and his recent unusual behavior. Since the Friday before, when our ordeal began, he had not said a word nor asked a question. He had gradually become more and more aloof and detached. Whenever we returned home after our hours of fruitless searching, Bardia would hurry toward me, glance at me curiously, and then, before I uttered a word, retreat dejectedly to a secluded corner of the house, where he would sit silently for hours. I could see his once-sparkling vitality withering away, turning him into a lifeless body looking for its missing soul.

• • • • •

That Friday, at around noon, Amin had come out of his office on Military College Street and disappeared. No one had seen him since, except for Soudabeh, his secretary, whom he had driven home to Alborz Street. Amin would have then driven south toward his father's house, where his father, Hajji Hedayatollah Jalali, our kids, and I were all waiting for him.

•   •   •   •   •

Together with Amin's family and friends, I had walked the short distance between this house and Alborz Street several times, asking the passers-by, shopkeepers, and the children loitering in front of the houses, "Did you see a gray Mercedes passing through this area at about noon last Friday?"

We had also shown them an eight-by-twelve color photograph of Amin, in which he was wearing a dark blue jacket and a striped tie and smiling at the camera. "Did you see this guy last Friday?"

•   •   •   •   •

The only positive response had come from an elderly woman who could barely see where she was going. She had looked at the portrait and said, "Yes, I think I saw him buying some fruits from Mash Taghi."

"Where? Where did you see him, dear?" Nargess had asked, despite her reluctance to believe the elderly woman's words.

"I saw him there. He was standing in front of Mash Taghi's shop, buying some fruit."

Her bony finger, pointing to the small shop on the other side of the road, was fixed in the air for a few moments.

Mash Taghi could not remember having seen Amin. He looked at the portrait and smiled, "It's been at least a year since I last saw such a well-dressed fellow around here. Yes. I'm positive. I have not seen him. How on earth would I forget such a man?"

I hastily interrupted him.

"But my husband was not wearing these clothes last Friday. He had a blue-striped shirt, and his trousers were gray."

The shopkeeper smiled at me. I knew that he, like other Iranians who first heard me speaking their language, must have thought that I was an Armenian. Armenians spoke Persian with an accent.

"Of course Madam. I know that such a portrait would not be recent. But I'm talking about the man himself. It's his features and style that I wouldn't forget."

There were at least a dozen children who claimed to have seen the gray Mercedes. One of them even said that the gray car had hit a green Peugeot.

During that week, there were 130 minor and eleven major accidents in Tehran, resulting in seven injuries and two deaths. But a gray Mercedes was not involved in any of them. Abdol and his wife, Soraya, had gone to visit two of the unidentified injured men, both comatose, in the hospital, but neither of them was Amin. Police had already informed us of the accidents and had told us that no one by the name of Dr. Amin Jalali, or a similar name, was hospitalized during that week.

On the third day of searching, while we discussed what the police had told us, Saeed repeated an unpleasant question he had brought up before.

"What if the police themselves have done this?"

The first time Saeed had brought up the issue, Hajji had rejected the idea furiously, and no one else had dared to bring it up again. This time it was my turn to open my swollen eyelids to cast a reproachful glance at him.

"But why? Why would the police arrest him so secretly? He couldn't have done anything wrong. He was not involved in any anti-Revolutionary activity, was he?"

"No. I know that. But these days, when they arrest someone, it does not necessarily mean that the person is guilty. They arrest people if they have the slightest suspicion," Saeed replied.

Abdol did not agree. He looked away from Saeed.

"Where do you get these ideas?" he said. "You don't have any clue."

Saeed answered him with his usual response.

"They are arresting people by the hundreds. But you have closed your eyes and ears to reality."

Abdol looked at him as if he were a little child in need of some fatherly lecture.

"Those are anti-Revolutionaries. Amin gave up all political activities years ago. They wouldn't arrest someone without reason."

Then he moved angrily away from Saeed and came toward me.

"Don't listen to him, Luba. Who could have anything against Amin?"

Who indeed? Amin was the son of Hajji Jalali, a man who had supported the Revolution from its onset and had spent millions of his own dollars for its victory. When Amin disappeared, Esmat Khanum, Hajji's wife, and Nargess, their daughter, had forced Hajji into action. Despite his age and the chaotic condition of his mind due to the disappearance of his son, Hajji had contacted and grilled everybody who was anybody in Tehran: members of the provisional government, members of the Revolutionary Court, police chiefs and, especially, the powerful leaders of the Revolutionary Committees. All of the men had declared their respect for Hajji and had assured him that they would never harm any member of his family. Even the head of Tehran's Central Police had personally asked Hajji to provide a photo of Amin to be printed in the evening papers.

Indeed, the following day, next to the Foreign Minister's words about the alleged cooperation of Shahpour Bakhtiar (the Shah's last prime minister) with Americans, one could see a six-by-four photo of Amin, this time without either a tie or a smile. The telephone numbers underneath the photo were that of the police. They later informed us that no one had answered their call for witnesses.

Friends and relatives telephoned my home to ask for more information or to console. In fact, it was one of them, a friend of Ahmad and an employee of the central morgue, who suggested that we should look at the unidentified corpses.

"It's wise to check the morgue, too. God forbid he should be there, but you might get some peace of mind. People take a lot of unidentified corpses there every day. The bodies are kept there until identified and claimed."

I, too, had thought of visiting the morgue on the day the police told us that there was no one resembling Amin in the hospitals. But I had not dared suggest so to others. Nevertheless, as soon as Ahmad timidly suggested the idea, I agreed.

• • • • •

Saeed and Abdol looked over more corpses than Ahmad. After his eighteenth corpse — a young man in his twenties — Ahmad could not move any further. He froze, with his hand clenching the green material stretched across the corpse. The young man, with his smashed nose turned into two uneven holes and his lips torn up to his left ear, seemed to sleep in tranquility. His face was completely clean. There was no blood, not even around his nose and lips. It was as if he had been born with that mask.

Finally, Ahmad managed to let the green cover drop over the face. He moved towards the nearest wall and leaned against the white tiles.

"I don't want to see anymore," he said.

Abdol saw that Ahmad's face had turned pale.

"You'd better leave."

Ahmad leaned his forehead on the tiles, but their coldness immediately made him pull back. A shiver ran across his shoulders.

"I don't want to see anymore."

"Okay. Don't look. Let's go outside."

Abdol and Saeed had led him to an adjacent room where a doctor was in attendance.

Saeed and Abdol had looked at another hundred and forty corpses: bodies with split foreheads, shapeless faces with protruding eyes, mouths torn out, ears plucked. But, fortunately — or unfortunately — Amin was not among them. The bodies mostly belonged to former SAVAK agents (the Shah's secret police) and the so-called anti-Revolutionaries.

This is what they were told by their guide as they went from one corpse to another. There was no anger or sorrow in his voice, but there was no joy either. In his oversized white uniform and large slippers, which made a creaking sound as he crossed the room, he seemed totally detached. Every now and then he would remove a cover, peek at a body, and utter a comment.

"This one must have been a member of SAVAK. Others are not killed in this way.... I've never seen an old man killed in such a manner. He must have been an anti-Revolutionary.... Look. They have cut off this one's hands. When they brought him here, there was a note attached to his coat saying that he was an anti-Revolutionary writer.... This one has no tongue. They have cut it off. He must have been a spy...."

.2.

Saeed drove us from the central morgue to Ferdowsi Square, where he dropped off Abdol. No one said a word during the entire ride. I was sitting in the back seat with my face exposed to the open window. The dry, hot wind which lashes the afternoons of Tehran burned my face. My eyes were stinging. Although I had closed my eyelids, the wind penetrated inside and scratched the surface of my eyes, already sore from tears.

Tehran cried for the cool breeze which was to come with the evening. Less than six months had passed since the victory of the Revolution and the change of government. The half-burnt and ruined buildings, the fallen trees, and the broken windows of the government offices were reminiscent of that outraged crowd which, with stones and bricks in their hands and froth on their lips, had brought about the victory. But now, the same crowd passed through the streets, separated and scattered, calm and tired, with lazy arms and feet, like runners who pass the finish line and search for a corner in which to sit and catch their breath, before they know who the winners are.

My mind was not working clearly. Even before Saeed said, "He is not here," I was already miles away. I had thought about my children. What should I say to Bardia if his father is found at central morgue? What should I do? Where should I go? I had thought about going back to London. I remembered the first time I met Amin there. I remembered our marvelous walks through the misty narrow streets of late September evenings. I revisited those secret short cuts in Hampstead Heath and that old, tall tree with its roots scattered all over the ground.

"Whenever I see this tree, I feel that a few more inches of its roots have come out of the ground. It's as if they're tired of living under the soil. They've come out to get nourishment, not from the earth, but from the sky," Amin once said. I realized that I could not possibly go back to London without Amin. But how would I live in Tehran without him? I could only answer myself with another question: "But where? Where should I go? Where can I go?"

But now my mind had stopped working. During those first few days, and whenever the possibility of Amin's death was brought up, my mind churned ceaselessly. My heart sank. I felt a shooting pain in every cell of my body. And I wept. I cried loudly in private. Throughout such moments, however, my mind was still working. Now, although the possibility of Amin's death did cause me to think about my children's future, my inability to decide whether Amin was dead or alive paralyzed my mind. I merely sat and looked around aimlessly, as if in a total vacuum.

Nargess sat next to me in the car, leaning back with her long hair, tied in a cream-colored clip. The tail of her hair was scattered on the back cushion. I knew that her mind, unlike mine, was busily working at that moment. She had the restless mind of a detective. Since Amin's disappearance, she had looked for every minor clue. She had followed every one of them, and, whenever faced with a dead-end, she would return to the beginning to follow another clue with the same fervor. At this particular moment, she was ruminating over the woman for whose sake Amin had gone to his office on that Friday, a day of the Iranian weekend. She spoke her mind loudly.

"We should try to find that woman. Whoever she is, she cannot be totally unrelated to Amin's disappearance. She may lead us to other important information."

No one answered. We all knew that there was no significant information about the patient. Even Soudabeh, the only person who had seen her, knew very little about her. The woman had entered the office around 9:30 a.m., said a few words to Amin, and had her abortion. After half an hour's rest, she had left the building. Soudabeh also remembered seeing, from the window of the office waiting room, a man sitting in a car in front of the building. She had thought that he was waiting for the woman.

He could have been the same friend who had referred the woman to Amin. Amin had told me about him last Friday morning, when I was lying in bed, watching Amin put on his blue-striped shirt.

"She was referred to me by a friend. She comes from a respectable family. If they find out about her situation, it will ruin her life."

"Where are you going?" Ahmad asked Saeed.

I noticed Ahmad's tired, drained profile. His eyes were still as dazed as when he had come out of the morgue. Saeed looked at him.

"To Hajji's place. Do you want me to take you home?"

"No, no. I'll come with you," Ahmad responded hastily. It was evident that he did not want to be left alone at home. But I longed to go home, to be far from everything for a while. I had stayed with my in-laws since the previous Friday and could not bear to see their sorrowful faces any more.

"Would it be possible for you to take me home?" I asked.

"If my parents do not see you with us, they'll get really nervous," Nargess responded. "You could come for a short while and then either Saeed or I will take you home."

My eyes caught Saeed's in the mirror. He was staring at me. He quickly looked away and accelerated the car. His mood reminded me of the way he acted during the night when he sat across from me at the Black Horse Pub in London. That night, I had told him about my life, my homeland, my mother, who was a famous singer, her suicide, which left me shattered at seventeen, my short-lived marriage to Milan, and my beloved father, whose blood-covered body I had found in his back garden the same day Milan and I had finally separated. My words were mixed with tears and sobs. Then, after a long pause, and while I was wiping my eyes, I caught Saeed's eyes, staring at me in total bewilderment. He was young and shy, and I had totally disarmed him by looking at him unexpectedly. He began aimlessly to rattle his glass on the table.

"You'll spill your beer," I said. Saeed let go of the glass and put his hands under his arms.

"Unbelievable. I can hardly imagine that Communists could be that harsh and cruel. It is unbelievable," he had said.

"Why are you driving so fast?" Ahmad shouted anxiously.

"I'm sorry. I was just thinking…. I don't know…. Where can he be? Where can we go next?"

Nargess took a deep breath and put her head on my shoulder.

"I told you. We have to find that woman."

Surrendering my shoulder to her, I rested my head against the window and asked, "But how?"

Apart from our small group, no one else was aware of that woman, not even the police. A total ban on abortion, although not yet legally enforced, was one of the first directives put in action after the revolution. Doctors who helped women abort their children were tried in the revolutionary courts. Therefore, we were unable to tell the police about the woman. And this was hindering our efforts to find her.

Nargess sat up and turned her face toward me. "How many friends could Amin have? We can ask all of them. We can ask those doctors who used to send their patients to Amin. One of them could be the one we're looking for. Someone like Dr. Jahangiri."

"But he left Iran two weeks ago," I said.

"We can ask Soudabeh to give us the names of all of Amin's professional contacts," Nargess said, still looking at me. "This is so very simple."

Saeed responded in a calm tone.

"Do you think that anyone would be willing to talk about this? They couldn't, even if they wanted to. It would mean that the woman would have to confront us. Look at the secrecy with which this abortion was carried out. She won't accept the risk of exposing herself."

Then came a moment of silence. I looked out and saw that we were passing by the museum. I realized that I had not been to work for six days. For a moment, I felt that I missed those ancient marvels housed inside the building. But immediately I felt ashamed of being concerned about them in such a situation.

"We have to do this," Nargess was saying. "Today, when we get home, I'll call Soudabeh."

I am not sure, even now, after so many years, whether I would have wished to find that woman, had Nargess not been so persistent while we were in the car. But I know it was from that day that the wish to find that woman planted a seed in my heart that began to grow rapidly into a stout tree—a tree so strong that even the disclosure of that woman's identity could not make it wither away. Still, after so many years, I search for a nameless woman in my dreams who is capable of disclosing a secret; perhaps a secret about my mother's suicide, or my father's murder, or Milan's sudden decision to divorce me. Sometimes she can make Amin appear on that height of Hampstead Heath, where a silver plaque tells you the name of all the faraway buildings. Sometimes she can keep him forever in the world of the lost people. She can take away my children or give them back to me. She can take me back to my own country or forever deprive me of the right to go there. She can blow up Stalin's huge monument on top of the Vancess Las Square and bring Dubcek back to power, or she can build hundreds of other statues all over the world. She can ....

.3.

We did not need to say anything. Esmat Khanum, Amin's mother, read our faces and knew immediately that we had not brought any news. She swallowed the lump in her throat and looked at the maid, who was standing in the doorway and watching us anxiously.

"Sedigheh Khanum, go and bring a few glasses of cold sherbet. Look in on the children as well," she said.

Then she made her heavy body comfortable in a maroon chair.

"The children are so happy today. Soraya and Homeira have brought their children here and they are all playing together. Why are you standing? Sit and make yourselves comfortable. You need a cold drink. What hellish weather!"

I knew that she was even more thirsty than we were for something cold to drink, but her religious zeal prevented her from consuming a beverage. It was Ramadan, the holy month of fasting during which Muslims are not allowed to eat or drink between sunrise and sunset.

We all sat down except Nargess, whose tall and well proportioned body bore no resemblance to her mother's. She spoke from where she stood in front of Esmat Khanum.

"Where is Dad?" she asked.

"He went to his office in the Bazaar. He was restless and thought it would help him if he concentrated on his work for a while."

"Don't you want to call Soudabeh?" Ahmad asked Nargess, with his eyes fixed on her.

Bewildered, Esmat Khanum looked at me.

"Did you find out anything new?"

"No, Mother. We want to get a list of Amin's doctor friends so we can call them," Nargess said, moving toward the telephone that rested on the little table between her mother and me.

I started to get up from my seat, but she put her hand on my shoulder and said, "Relax. I'll use the phone in the other room."

I did not feel relaxed at all. I never felt relaxed in that room. It was half lit and had a heavy, stale atmosphere. I looked at the small window behind the thick green velvet curtains, which was the only bright spot in the room. I hated that room. It was filled with so many bits of contrasting furniture that it reminded me of the second-hand shops on London's Portobello Road. There were heavy green and maroon sofas all over the place. Cupboards were overstuffed with pieces of china and silverware. In every corner, various chairs and small tables were covered by numerous crystal vases that reminded me of where I came from.

The first day I entered that room, Amin had said, "These vases are made in Czechoslovakia."

"What a strange room!" I had said.

"I thought you'd like it. Everything here is old."

"If I were an antique dealer I might have liked it."

I had immediately regretted what I had said. I didn't know why I spoke so bitterly and it would have been understandable if Amin had been displeased. He did not say anything that day, but from then on, whenever we visited his parents, he would persuade everyone to gather in the living room or the television room. These rooms were furnished according to Nargess's taste and contained modern furniture. Although I still thought that the high ceilings covered with plaster moldings, as well as the old ornamented wooden doors, did not match the modern furniture, I did like the bright and cheerful atmosphere of those rooms.

Before I could sip my drink, Bardia and Bahram came running into the room. Bahram rambunctiously jumped into my arms and Bardia, with his head tilted to the side, calmly sat on the arm of my chair and looked at me with his soft hazel eyes. His eyes looked sunken and his face was pale. I ruffled his smooth acorn-colored hair, which he had inherited from me. He always liked it when I did that. But this time, he moved away and looked down. Bahram jumped up and down on my lap and asked his usual questions.

"Is Daddy coming back today?"

"No, dear. I told you. He's away on a trip."

"When is he coming back? Tomorrow?"

"Could be tomorrow, could be later...."

Esmat Khanum wiped her eyes with the back of her hand and opened her arms wide. "Come here, my little boy. Come here and let your mother drink her sherbet."

Bahram was reluctant to go. Saeed stood up and held him gently in his arms. "Come and tell your uncle what you have been up to today. You must tell me everything."

Nargess returned and kissed Bardia on the cheek.

"Soudabeh is free. She can come with us to the office," she told us. Then she moved toward Bardia, who was silently leaving the room. She grasped him in her arms. "How is my precious Bardia?"

Bardia, smiling shyly, let Nargess kiss his face and murmured, "I'm fine, Auntie."

He left the room. Esmat Khanum, her eyes filled with love, watched him walk out the door.

"He is so much like his father," she said wistfully. "When Amin was fourteen, he was the same height. Everyone thought he was seventeen. He had the same calmness. I remember the day when...."

My eyes momentarily interlocked with Saeed's. Then I lowered my head with shame, as I did whenever someone talked about the resemblance of Bardia and Amin in front of my husband's family. Besides Amin and myself, Saeed was the only one who knew that Bardia had no blood relations with this family. I saw Amin as my accomplice in this lie, but what about Saeed? I was sure about his integrity and faithfulness. I was sure that he would keep this secret to himself, as he had always done. But I could not get rid of the anxiety of knowing that he was one of only three people aware of this secret, the disclosure of which would immediately change the position of Bardia in this family. Bardia, the first son of Dr. Amin Jalali, the first grandson of Hajji Hedayatollah Jalali, the apple of my in-laws' eyes, would become a Bardia who had a Czech father named Milan and was therefore completely alien to this family. This would be a very embarrassing fact in a traditional and wealthy Iranian family such as the Jalalis.

Bardia was barely a week old when Amin had proposed to me. He had decided to tell his family and friends that we had got married a year before and Bardia was our son. I was glad that, in this way, my son would have a father and a large family. Nevertheless, I could not understand why my husband's family should react unfavorably if they were told that Bardia was not their real grandson. The answer only became clear to me later on, after I learned about Iranian society and attitudes during my stay in Iran. Had Amin taken another course of action, Bardia would have been received as a guest and not as a true member of the family. Such a guest would certainly be showered by Iranian hospitality and kindness, but he would not be considered as an integral part of the household. Once, when I commented about this complicated situation, Amin became annoyed.

"I don't understand why you think about this so much," he said. "I hardly remember that Bardia isn't my real son. He's just not related to me by blood, that's all. Apart from that, there's no difference between him and a real son. Do you think I love him less than Bahram? Is my behavior somehow different toward him?"

My answer could not be but a negative one. Before Bahram was born, I sometimes thought that if Amin was to have a son of his own it might change his attitude towards Bardia. Perhaps it was due to this fear that I rejected the idea of having another child for seven years.

But, contrary to my doubts, Bahram's birth did not change anything. Amin continued to behave like a real father to Bardia; like a loving father, to be precise. For Bardia, Amin was someone to look up to. He imitated Amin in every way and did everything his father requested.

"Bardia has inherited everything from Amin," Amin's family members often repeated. No one paid any attention to the fact that Bardia's eyes and hair resembled mine. And no one knew that his short nose and bony cheeks were genetic copies of his real father's features. They talked about his tall stature, which was similar to Amin's; they pointed to the way he walked, which was as calm and dignified as Amin's gait. His patience and serenity seemed to replicate Amin's demeanor, and his voice, deep and warm, echoed Amin's way of speaking.

That day, Esmat Khanum was again talking about the similarities between Amin and Bardia, but she was interrupted by the telephone. She picked up the receiver with her fat hand, from which dangled a collection of gold bracelets.

"Hello? That's right, this is Hajji Agha's residence.... No, he's not home.... Who's speaking?"

She listened for a while and then, with a faint voice and a pale face, waved the receiver at Saeed.

"He says he wants to talk to a man."

Before Saeed could move, Nargess grabbed the receiver from her mother.

"Can I help you? I am Hajji Agha's daughter. He is not home at the moment. You can tell me whatever you want to tell him. It makes no difference. If you have anything to say, say it to me!"

Her voice was powerful and commanding and one could tell that the man at the other end had surrendered to its force. She fell silent and listened carefully. Her face became grim and turned red before becoming totally pale. Esmat Khanum leaned toward Nargess with wide eyes, as if she were on the verge of bursting into loud sobs. The sentence "I want to talk to a man" signaled the worst. In Iran they always break bad news first to the men, because of the belief that males are stronger and can take the news more easily. I, too, knew this and was invaded by a rush of sudden anxiety. I felt my heart blowing up like a balloon and rapidly ascending toward my throat. My eyes moved rapidly back and forth between Nargess and Esmat Khanum. I listened to Nargess carefully.

"At what time? Yes.... Yes.... Are you sure? Can I see you for a minute? Please.... Listen, I...."

I could hear the click as the line was cut at the other end. Nargess looked at the receiver for a moment with bewilderment.

"What is it, Nargess? What did he say?" Esmat Khanum asked her in a muffled voice.

Nargess put the receiver down and, with an evident effort to show that nothing serious had happened, answered, "Nothing Mother."

"Tell me the truth, Nargess! What's happened?"

"Nothing, Mother. I swear to God. He said that he saw Amin last Friday. But he seemed to be a prank caller."

Esmat Khanum leaned back, and her harsh voice, mixed with her heavy breath, filled the room.

"Damn those people!"

She seemed to be relieved. But I felt that there was something more substantial in what Nargess had heard. She seemed anxious and uneasy. At the same time, I could tell that the caller did not relay news of Amin's death. My thoughts were confirmed when Nargess looked at Saeed and said, "We'd better go pick up Soudabeh. She's waiting for us. We should not waste time."

She took her car keys out of her pocket and gave them to Ahmad.

"Could you take Luba and the children home? We'll join you later on."

Saeed, still curiously watching Nargess, put Bahram down and moved toward the door.

I was left with many unanswered questions. Ahmad was drowning in his deep thoughts and Esmat Khanum was preparing herself for another round of her long monologues. I knew that it would take her another two hours before she set us free. I could not find enough energy for such an ordeal.

Although she often bored me, in hindsight I realize that I very much liked my mother-in-law. She was one of the few women educated in Iran who had gone to school after the advent of the liberal Iranian Constitutional Revolution at the turn of the century. She was born in Tabriz, a city in the northwest of Iran. During the Constitutional Revolution, the men of her family had fought against the religious extremists who advocated the rule of the clergy over the newly formed Parliament.

As a young woman, she herself was involved in the societies and activities of progressive women in the 1920s — a lifestyle that demanded courage at that time. During the modernizations of the Shah's father, she had been one of the first women to give up wearing the traditional veil, or "chador." When she was twenty years old, she began her career as a teacher at a girls' school. A few years later, she married Hajji Jalali, who was not a religious man at that time and so did not have the honorable title, "Hajji." Muslims may use this title only after they make the pilgrimage to the holy city of Mecca in Saudi Arabia.

Esmat Khanum could not remember how or when her inclinations towards religion had begun. She used to explain that she had worn her scarf after Hajji's pilgrimage to Mecca out of respect for his new social position. She was forty-one when she volunteered for retirement. Then she went to Mecca and, upon her return, began to wear the veil again.

Several times, she had told me the story of how she had managed to get the authorities to accept her retirement application. She talk about herself as if she were referring to someone else.

She once told me, "To be honest with you, I did not like the idea of becoming a housewife for good. But when Nargess became ill, I panicked. She caught a dangerous disease and needed a lot of care. Three out of five of my children died at birth, and I was left only with Amin and Nargess, who were thus all the more dear to me. If it weren't for them, Hajji's insistence that I leave my job would not have influenced me."

From the early months of our arrival in Iran, whenever we visited Hajji and Esmat Khanum, she would sit next to me and talk for hours. Through her, I came to know every member of that extended family, as well as whatever they had done and thought. Of course, she expected me to talk to her in the same way. She wanted me to tell her about my past, my family, and my country, but I was always reluctant to do so. It was simple to evade her wishes. I merely answered her questions by throwing some new questions back at her, so she would immediately return to her long-winded monologues. In the beginning, she believed that I had difficulty expressing myself in Persian but, later on, she noticed that I spoke the language fluently and was able to say whatever I wanted. Therefore, she had come to the conclusion that I was particularly reluctant to talk to her. She had mentioned this fact several times to me. "It's always me doing the talking. You always just listen. Exactly like Hajji. I so wish he would talk to me about… about anything, about his concerns or, at least, about whatever happens in his office at the Bazaar. But, alas, nothing. Not even a few words!"

I knew that she liked me. Our calm and stable life made her happy. She saw a resemblance between her life and mine.

"You and Amin always remind me of our own youth," She once said. Then she laughed and continued, "Of course, in those days I was not so talkative. When I became a housewife, I gradually became more and more talkative. I don't know why I like to talk so much. I worry about everything. Sometimes I even enjoy grumbling for no apparent reason!"

Sometimes she believed that having come closer to God had opened her eyes and raised her expectations. She thought that Nargess had become ill to remind her of her duties toward God; staying at home had given her the chance to get closer to Him. She was an interesting woman, an example of most of the well-to-do Iranian women. She was a kind, devoted mother and, at the same time, a loquacious person. There was no ambiguity or complexity in her behavior. And although no one cared to pay much attention to what she said, Esmat Khanum still insisted on being informed of whatever happened to her husband, children, and the small world around her.

.4.

After I put the children to bed, I placed a bottle of vodka on the kitchen table. Following the revolution, production and consumption of alcohol had been entirely banned; thus, the bootleggers had a lucrative business. The day before Amin's disappearance, I had obtained the vodka from an acquaintance who illegally produced alcoholic spirits.

Ahmad was pacing in the living room and I could see him each time he passed the large door that connected the room to the kitchen. I asked him to join me in the kitchen for a drink. Ahmad sat down across from me and glanced at his watch.

"Aren't they late?"

I was worried, as well. The air in the apartment was heavy with tension. Despite the ever presence of Amin in every corner of the apartment, I still felt more comfortable in my own home. I knew that I had annoyed Hajji and his wife by insisting on going back home, but I simply didn't have the energy to stay any longer. This was my own home and I loved every bit of it. The first moment I entered my apartment on a bright autumn afternoon, I knew that I was at home. It was quite different from most Iranian homes. It was a spacious apartment with large, bright rooms and wide windows in a modern and newly built residential complex located in the heart of Amirieh, a traditional district of Tehran. I liked the kitchen most of all. A large door opened into a balcony overlooking Amirieh Street, which, dotted with tall plane trees, extended far into the landscape. I could see the Alborz Mountains in the north of Tehran with the tall peak, Towchal, towering above the horizon. On the left, the western landscape of Tehran was covered with dust and smoke. The first night we moved into the new apartment, I asked Amin if we could have our dinner on the balcony. Although the weather was chilly, we sat there for hours and looked at Tehran, wrapped in a dark blanket with scores of twinkling lights woven into its fabric.

I stood up and opened the balcony doors. The coolness of Tehran's summer evening gently touched my face. I returned to my seat opposite Ahmad, who was lighting a cigarette. On a sudden impulse, I asked him for one. Ahmad, totally astonished, offered the cigarette box. He had not seen me smoke a cigarette during the three and half years in which he had lived in the neighboring apartment. I inhaled the smoke deep into my lungs and tried to explain.

"Before I had Bahram, I used to smoke. After that I quit."

Ahmad said nothing, but I could see him gazing at me from behind the muslin curtain of smoke. His expression was filled with emptiness. Three months later, he would show me one of his paintings that described what was going on in his head during that night. A big bluish-white fish lay motionless on a seashore with its large glazed eyes reflecting the sky and the sea. Two uneven holes under one eye led to torn lips. A drop of blood oozed from the left gill.

He came back to his senses as I poured him his second drink. He raised his head and looked at me.

"Am I bothering you?" he asked in a low, shy voice.

"Oh, not at all. I'm so happy that you're here. I'm glad that Amin and I have such nice friends. I think I'd go mad if I were left alone."

Would I really go mad if I were left alone? What if Amin was going to die or was already dead? This time it was my turn to leave Ahmad and travel back to somewhere far away; to the house where I found my father's body soaked in blood on the gravel-walk of its tiny garden and, losing my control, screamed and screamed. But when I saw so many frightened faces peering at me sheepishly from behind the curtains of their windows, I stopped. I knew that I could not rely on the help of people who used to shun us as if we had the plague.

I took my father's hands and dragged him into the kitchen through the small door. I washed from his face the blood that had spilled from two holes on top of his left brow. Then, weeping, I put a pillow under his head.

"Please forgive me," I said in a muted voice. "I won't stay in this hell any longer."

Throughout those moments, I thought to myself, "If I do not go mad, I will be able to escape from Prague. If I stay cool, I may even be able to get out of Czechoslovakia." And I did. But I always believed that if I had had a friend or a relative to talk to, everything would have been more bearable.

"When they killed my father, I was really lonely. For a long time no one dared to come near us," I said, unintentionally.

Ahmad was caught by surprise and tried to show some kind of supportive reaction. "Tell me... was your father an anti-communist?" he asked.

During the three and half years in which Ahmad had become our friend, he had tried several times to talk to me about my country and its recent history. A week after he rented the apartment next to ours, Amin invited him for supper. It was during that night that we realized that Ahmad had definite socialist inclinations. But he effectively concealed them from others until the beginning of the upheavals preceding the revolution. From the time I had married Amin, and especially since our arrival in Iran, I had refrained from discussing my country to avoid mentioning the fate of my family.

Amin had told me that besides a handful of people who studied in Europe and were attracted to Communist organizations in their youth, most Iranians hated the left and were very sensitive to anyone with leftist inclinations. In fact, this sensitivity was quite evident in Amin himself. Without losing his calm, he would talk about the struggles of Iranians to nationalize their oil resources during the premiership of Mohammed Mossadegh in the early fifties. He would point out the treachery of Tudeh Party (the Iranian pro-Soviet Communist Party) and, in doing so, he aimed to refute all socialist doctrines with a single stroke. He would always add emphatically that he wouldn't talk about other countries and what Communism could do for them, but in the case of Iran, he said the result would be devastating and impossible to remedy.

I had learned not to participate in political discussions and had even come to accept that others would inevitably interpret my escape from Czechoslovakia as an escape from all forms of Communism. Whenever someone asked about my nationality, Amin would answer for me.

"Luba comes from Czechoslovakia," he'd say. "She actually escaped from that country!"

Even after the Shah's departure from Iran, an act that increased political freedoms and resulted in open activities by Leftist groups, my position did not change. I could see clearly that educated people, students, and government employees, as well as a large section of the labor force, were inclined towards the "Independent Left," which referred to those socialists who were against the communism imported from Moscow. Even those people who were against the acceptance of the independent leftists in the government did not deny their sincerity and acknowledged their contributions towards the freedom of Iran. Nevertheless, the new situation had further fueled Amin's anger and the fury of those among his friends who shared his political views; friends such as Dr. Jahangiri and Dr. Dowlatian. I did not wish to antagonize him. Many times, heated debates arose, with Amin and his friends on one side, and Nargess, Saeed, Abdol, and Ahmad on the other. I would remain silent or leave the room with some excuse. Within the group, Saeed was the only one who knew that I did not share Amin's political views. But it seemed that he also had accepted that I was not to be involved in any political debate. In fact, since the first few months of my arrival in London, during which I frequently discussed my political views with Saeed, I had never again returned to that topic.

"No. My father was not against Communism. But he did not agree with the puppet government planted by the Soviets. He began his political activities years before Dubcek came to power."

Ahmad gazed at me with his gray eyes, now wide open with amazement.

"Did you support Dubcek as well?"

I poured another glass for myself. I was feeling drunk for the first time in many years. I also regretted starting the discussion in the first place. I took another cigarette and Ahmad, waiting for my answer, lit it for me. I answered him with a nod.

"But so many years have passed since those days. When I escaped from my country, I was only nineteen. After that, I don't know anything about whatever has happened there. I'm not even interested in knowing anymore."

I was lying. I was indeed curious about any news related to my country. With Ahmad, however, I was trying to find an end to an unwanted dialogue I had begun unintentionally. Fortunately, before Ahmad could say anything else, the doorbell rang. Although before our discussion, Ahmad had glanced at his watch quite frequently, now he did not seem very excited to hear the doorbell. He reluctantly stood up and began to walk toward the door.

"I have always been very curious about Dubcek and his views on socialism," he said. "We should sit and talk about it again sometime. I have lots of questions to ask you."

With one look at Nargess, I immediately knew that something had happened. The two oblique lines drawn from the sides of her nostrils to the corner of her lips always betrayed her feelings. When she was happy, they disappeared, and her nostrils exhibited their well-curved form. But whenever she was sad or deeply involved in an inner conflict, they resurfaced. At that moment, I had never seen those lines so deep.

After she and Saeed sat down, Nargess explained that they had made a list of doctors who used to send their patients to Amin. Saeed was to contact all of them. We were silent for a while. Then, as if trying to change the subject, she took three envelopes out of her bag and put them on the table.

"These letters were in the mailbox at Amin's office."

I looked at the letters. Two from England and one from France. Each was addressed to Amin. I put them aside and looked at Nargess.

"Tell me. What was that phone call about?"

Nargess shrugged and asked for a cup of tea. While I prepared the tea with my back to my friends, I heard Nargess's voice, which sounded different than usual.

"I couldn't say it in front of my mother. The man on the telephone said that he had seen the Revolutionary Guards arrest Amin at 12:30 on Friday. He told me details about Amin that he would not have known had he not seen him with his own eyes."

My hands trembled. I did not know what kind of expression my face was supposed to display when I eventually had to turn and face them. The alcohol had not left me much control.

I heard Ahmad ask, "What sort of details?"

"Things like what Amin was wearing, where he had dropped off Soudabeh, and what Soudabeh was wearing. And other similar things."

I turned toward them and, putting the cups on the table, asked Nargess, "Couldn't it be that he had seen all these things but was fabricating the story of Amin's arrest?"

Ahmad shook his head in a childish manner.

"Right. This could be the case."

Silence prevailed once again. Nargess and Saeed's silence worried me. I sensed that they had a lot more information about Amin's arrest. I looked at them inquisitively. Saeed's head was bent downwards and his fingers were drawing some invisible lines on the table. Nargess, refusing to look me in the eye, shifted her shoulders.

"I don't know. To be honest with you, I can't think anymore."

This was the first time I had heard her say such a thing. I had never seen her look so defeated. I had to wait about five months before she would eventually tell me what had happened to her — and to me. I have never forgiven her for those five months of being kept in the dark. On the other hand, I have never been able to speculate what other course of action I would have taken had they told me everything that night.

The silence that was repeatedly overshadowing our conversation finally brought our meeting to an end. Nargess complained about her headache and said that she needed some rest. She had decided to spend the night at my place and wanted to go to bed early. Saeed and Ahmad stood up to go.

I escorted them to the door. Ahmad opened his apartment door, said good night, and went inside. Saeed was still standing at the doorway, reluctant to leave. He was looking at me with worried eyes. Then he took my hands and softly said, "Luba. Take care of yourself. Everything will be all right."

I shook my head. He released my hands and reluctantly moved towards the stairs.

His mood was not new to me. For several months, he had fallen into a similar mood whenever he was supposed to go home. Once, he even told Amin and me, "Maggie's cold face makes me disgusted to go home."

Actually, both Amin and I had noticed a change in Maggie's attitude as well. It had been about a year since she had come to Iran and it had taken her only a month to turn into a sad and detached woman.

She was not the same energetic and talkative person whom I knew in England. Now she stayed at home all day and spent her time with her daughter, Lili. She seldom ventured outside and hardly accepted any invitations. Whenever Saeed invited others to their place, Maggie would sit for a while with the guests and then, sometimes even before the food was served, would apologize and go to bed. Once, in front of Amin and me, she told Saeed that he should not expect anything more from her and that her acceptance to come to Iran with Saeed was to be considered as her extreme sacrifice. Saeed had reminded her of the only condition he had put forward before their marriage.

"If you want to marry me you should accept the fact that one day or another I'll go back to Iran," he said. "It could be next month or next year or, perhaps, in ten years' time. But my future will definitely be in Iran."

He waited four more years before the dissatisfaction and disillusionment of the Iranian people with the dictatorship of the Shah created an explosive situation inside Iran. This change in political atmosphere alerted the American government, which considered Iran to be one of its major satellites. President Carter went to Iran to put pressure on the Shah to agree to a number of civil freedoms requested by the people. One of these liberties pertained to the Iranian students outside of the country who were involved in political activities against the Shah's regime.

Margaret and her two-year-old daughter joined Saeed two months after he returned to Iran. Upon their arrival, Margaret had laughingly confessed that she had never believed that Saeed, being so involved in anti-Shah activities, actually would be allowed to return to his country. Saeed had already rented a nice house in the Vanak area of Tehran. Vanak was located in the north of the capital and the petrodollars pouring into Iran in the 1970s had turned the area into a modern, affluent quarter of the city. Saeed was a successful architect in London and, on returning to Iran, easily found a good job in an architectural firm. His income was more than the sum of what he and Margaret each could earn in London.

Margaret and Saeed had met each other in the International Trotskyite Organization. They were both involved in most of the organization's activities and traveled to other countries for that reason. Saeed was under the impression that Margaret was interested in being personally involved with revolutionary activities in Third World countries; therefore, he thought she would be eager to experience Iran. During her first month in Iran, Margaret was exactly whom she was expected to be. She would go anywhere with Saeed and was interested in knowing everything she could about the country. Nargess had given her a few books that taught Persian to foreigners and had decided to help teach Margaret the language. She had done the same for me.

Although I had learned Persian before going to Iran, it was only because of her help that I could take examinations and receive my diploma in Persian. Margaret welcomed Nargess's assistance in the beginning. She was even employed in a bilingual school as an English teacher and was supposed to start teaching at the beginning of the following term. But, in a sudden change of heart, she dropped all of her plans and imprisoned herself at home. It was as if she had gone on a strike. I thought that she wanted to force Saeed to return the family to England, but she never uttered such a proposal to him. She did not even complain about anything.

She rejected invitations in a calm but most decisive way. "Sorry, honey, I don't want to go to your friend's home. But you can go if you like."

"Sorry, love, I'm tired and cannot entertain your guests."

"I'd prefer to stay home and do some gardening. You can take Lili to see your parents."

Saeed could sense a shadow looming over their life and so he was reluctant to go home. He knew that Margaret did not like living in Iran and merely tolerated the living arrangement for his benefit. But whenever he voiced this observation, Margaret denied it and protested.

"Have I said anything to make you think that? I am accustomed to our life in Iran now. Of course I'm doing this for your sake. But what is so bad about that?"

And Saeed did not know what to do.

He disappeared down the staircase. Completely drained of all senses and thoughts, I shut the door and leaned against it.

.5.

The next day, August the tenth, early in the morning, the ringing of the telephone awakened Nargess and me. It was Soraya. She and her husband, Abdol, lived near Hajji's house. She informed us that Amin, critically injured, was at Hajji's place.

There was no hint of joy in Soraya's voice, but I could not stop myself from shouting out of sheer delight. Amin was alive, our nightmare had come to an end, and everything could return to normal. I ran towards Ahmad's apartment and woke him up with a long, loud knock on his door. When he sleepily opened the door, I told him the news and asked if he'd watch my children until Fatemeh Khanum, the maid, arrived. Nargess and I then embarked to go to my in-laws' house.

Nargess did not utter a word during the entire ride. Once we reached my in-laws' house, before we even left the car, I could hear a male voice reciting a passage from Koran, the holy book of Muslims. His sorrowful voice poured out of the half-opened door of Hajji's house, infusing the Friday morning with a sad, heavy atmosphere. The house seemed rather crowded for so early on a weekend morning, as if people were mourning the death of a loved one. A few men, as well as some women wrapped in black veils, were standing in the hallway and murmuring to each other. Through the wide-open door in the hall, I could see a number of men sitting in the living room. The voice of the Koran reciter came from the same room. Then I saw my father-in-law, sitting amongst the other men, with his neck leaning to one side. He clutched a white handkerchief in his tightly clenched hand. But I could only think of Amin. Where was he?

• • • • •

At 3:30 that morning, Hajji was sitting in his bed after a long night of struggling with his thoughts. This was the time when everybody in the house was supposed to wake up and eat. The meal, called "sahari," constituted the last food any devoted Muslim could consume before the commencement of the day-long fasting period. Hajji always arose early, just before the morning call came from the Mohammed Mosque down the road; the call invited believers to wake up and recite their morning prayers. It was as if there was an invisible alarm clock ticking in his head. Esmat Khanum once told me that not a single day in Hajji's life had he woken up late for his morning prayers. No matter what, he always woke up right on time, as if someone prodded him awake. Hajji would sit and wait for the call from the mosque. Then he would turn to Esmat Khanum and gently wake her up:

"Esmat Khanum…. Esmat Khanum…. Wake up, my dear…. It's time for the morning prayers."

She would always wait for this ritual, even if she was already awake. But that day, Hajji had not done so. He knew that she too had had a troubled night and had hardly slept. Neither of them had slept comfortably, even for a few hours, throughout that week. Amin's disappearance had disturbed every aspect of their tranquil life.

They had lived together for forty-four years without any serious trouble. They had even gotten over the premature deaths of three children because of the joy of Amin's birth. Living separated from Amin for fifteen years had not disturbed their peaceful life, either. They missed him very much, but there was nothing worrisome about the separation. Whenever Esmat Khanum became depressed and cried over the son whom she did not get to see as often as she would have liked, Hajji consoled her by reminding her that Amin would return when he finished his studies. Whenever Esmat Khanum was restless, Hajji promised to take her to see her son. This calmed her, but at the same time, she knew that they would never go on that trip.

In truth, the couple wasn't interested in going to Europe, anyway. Their trips always had religious motivations. They would visit holy places out of religious duty or, as Saeed once said, in order to become more credible in the bazaar. In the main bazaar of Tehran, where most of the traditional trades of the country were centered, one could not gain any recognized credibility without having gone on religious pilgrimages to the holy places scattered in Saudi Arabia, Iraq, or Syria.

Hajji, as usual, got out of bed, went to the hall, and turned on the lights. In that early time of the day, the hall seemed brilliant under the light emanating from the crystal chandeliers. The reflection of the light on the crowded silverware inside the cupboards was eye-catching. Apart from a crystal bowl, two candlesticks, and a large tray that Esmat Khanum had brought with her as her dowry, the rest of the items were bought during the pair's married life. Even, after forty-four years, Esmat Khanum had not lost her penchant for buying silverware.

Hajji passed by the imprisoned silverware and opened the bathroom door. But before entering the bathroom, he heard the bell. It was a brief, muffled noise. He thought that it could have been made by the rusty hinges on the bathroom door. Nevertheless, he returned to the hall and went to the small landing in front of the entrance door. Through the tiny colored glasses he saw the shadow of someone standing behind the door. He wondered who could be calling on him so early in the morning. He felt his heart beating hard.

He hurriedly opened the locks; first one, then the next, then the third lock, which was connected to a safety chain. Behind the door, he saw the caretaker of the mosque staring at him with fear-stricken eyes. Hajji tried to read the eyes. The old man avoided his gaze and greeted him.

"Good morning Mashd Akbar. What do you want?" Hajji asked.

Instead of responding, the old man put his hands on his face and lowered his head. His trembling shoulders revealed that he was crying, hard and silent. Later on, townspeople would swear that, apart from the religious mourning during the month of Moharram in which, according to Shi'ite mythology, the martyrdom of the Prophet's nephews had occurred, no one had ever seen the old man cry until that morning.

"What's wrong, Mashd Akbar? Why don't you say anything?"

Hajji heard the old man, still with his faced covered in his hands, mutter something like "Amin Agha." Hajji leaned against the door, feeling the tremendous pressure of a heavy weight on his chest. He tried to ask, "What about Amin?" But he had completely lost his voice. Mashd Akbar took his hands off his face and looked at him with tearful eyes. He was shocked by Hajji's pale face. Wiping his eyes, he led Hajji back inside and groaned, "O great God. In you we trust."

He helped Hajji to rest on a couch near the window, and rushed into the kitchen for a glass of water. He lowered it to Hajji's lips and said, "Drink, Hajji Agha. Drink."

Hajji, neither taking the glass nor drinking from it, looked at the old man and, with a harsh voice said, "Tell me what has happened to Amin."

Mashd Akbar helplessly kneeled in front of him and again covered his face with his hands. He could not say what he wanted to say while looking Hajji in the eye.

"May God give you patience, sir…."

"Tell me what has happened to him. Tell me."

"May God give you patience. It is His wishes, sir. He has taken Amin Agha's life. He always calls his better men back sooner…."

Hajji's pale face suddenly flared up and a wild rush of blood flooded his deep wrinkles. A weak moan came from his lips, which repeated the call of the reciter from the mosque: "Allah is the greatest, Allah is the greatest."

Mashd Akbar heard Esmat Khanum calling Hajji from the other end of the corridor. Hajji looked helplessly at Mashd Akbar as if he had suddenly remembered her. Then he hit his forehead with the palm of his hand. Mashd Akbar stood up and went toward the door to the garden. He wanted to call Sedigheh Khanum and ask her to wake Nargess and any other women who might be in the house.

When he returned with Sedigheh Khanum, who was beating her head and chest, he saw the huge body of Esmat Khanum stretched motionless on the floor. Hajji was sitting near her head, caressing his wife's face and closed eyes and murmuring something that Mashd Akbar was unable to decipher.

● ● ● ● ●

Nargess, with a trembling voice, shouted, "Where is Amin?"

No one gave her an answer. The veiled women hastily led us toward the other room, where I could see Esmat Khanum and her sister, Nosrat Khanum, sitting between a few women dressed in black and wailing in their loudest voices. Spotting Nargess and me, Esmat Khanum shouted loudly and then fainted in her sister's arms. This was the third time she had fainted since Hajji had told her, "God give us patience. We have lost our son."

The other women in the room began to wail loudly in accompaniment. Nargess was trembling by the door. She looked for a while at her mother, who lay unconscious in her sister's arms and then, like a fragile tree branch exposed to a wild wind, collapsed onto the floor.

From the time Soraya's call had woken her up, Nargess had vaguely sensed that Soraya's news was graver than she had revealed. Nargess, like other Iranians, could understand the hidden meanings underlying such news. But I had believed what Soraya had told me. In my culture there was no need for disclosing bad news in a gradual manner and thus I could not comprehend why she would have hidden the truth from me. Now, even though it was obvious that Amin was dead, I could not believe it. Soraya read my feelings, took my arm and, while gently forcing me to sit down, murmured soothingly in English. "I'm sorry, Luba…. Abdol didn't want me to tell you over the phone. Amin is dead. I'm sorry."

I felt an intense twinge in my head. It was as if someone had driven a red hot needle from one temple to the other. My eyes were bursting under its pressure and pain. I tried to close them for a moment but I had no control. They were wandering desperately from Nargess to Esmat Khanum to the wailing women. Esmat Khanum had regained her consciousness and, while looking at me, repeatedly cried out, "Do you see, Luba dear, how we lost our dear Amin? Do you see how our dearest flower withered away?"

And the women shook their heads and beat their knees. I did not know some of them. They were mostly elderly women whose curious eyes, nailed into their wrinkled, pale, black-veiled faces, were fixed on me. Without blinking, they watched my every movement. They could not miss anything because they needed details so that they could narrate them later on.

One of them later told her daughter, a friend of Soraya, what she had observed.

"I had never seen such a thing in my life. These foreign women are really strange. She neither wept nor uttered a word. Her face was as pale as a dead face. She just watched every one of us. At first I thought that the shock had locked her tongue and tears. So I sat down next to her and told her, 'Try to weep Luba Khanum; it's good for you. Weep!' I was afraid that the shock might cause a stroke in her head or heart. She could die or go mad. But she did not weep at all.

She sat there for an hour and gazed at us. We all had practically forgotten poor Amin because we were so worried about her. Nargess came over to sit next to her. She put her arms around Luba and wept. Esmat Khanum spoke gentle and loving words. But Amin's wife just sat there and watched us. Then, suddenly, she stood up and went into the corridor. She told the men there, 'Take me to my husband. I want to see his body.'"

Saeed and Abdol took me to Nargess's room which was far from the other rooms and had a separate door opening toward the garden. They tried to convince me not to see Amin.

They said, "It is not custom here for a wife to see her husband's dead body." They were lying. They didn't want me to see my husband in such dreadful shape. Saeed and Abdol had seen the body a few hours before, when, at Hajji's insistence, they had taken him to the mosque.

• • • • •

Abdol believed that Hajji should not see his son. While Saeed had gone to see his aunt, Esmat Khanum, who was sitting with a few of the women, still stricken by the shock, Abdol had listened to what Mashd Akbar had to say about the body. He could guess from the old man's words that it would be difficult for Hajji to see his son in such a condition.

Early in the morning Mashd Akbar had awakened his son to prepare the food for the commencement of the fasting period. He himself had gone to open the mosque's door and sweep the entrance. He had performed the same duties since Hajji had built the Mohammed mosque twenty-one years ago and appointed him as the caretaker.

In the faint light of a lamp on the portal of the mosque, Mashd Akbar had seen a man sleeping on the pavement. He was not surprised. It could have been any beggar or stranger. Many such people came to Hajji's mosque. Hajji had allocated two rooms for such guests. They would stay in these rooms until they could find a job and somewhere else to live. They were Hajji's guests or, as Hajji used to call them, God's guests.

Mashd Akbar had gone to the sleeping man and had called him. Suddenly, he realized the man was Hajji Agha's son. He had recognized Amin not by his face but by his body. He told Abdol that Amin had been killed so brutally that one could not look at his face.

Hajji had insisted on seeing his son. They had taken him to the mosque and to the room where the bodies of the dead were usually kept until the break of dawn. Mashd Akbar's son and two local police officers were standing in front of the room. When Hajji arrived, they moved away to let him and his entourage enter the room. Hajji entered first, moving silently toward Amin's body which was hidden under a white cloth. A ray of light from the window illuminated the white sheet. Hajji kneeled down next to the body and calmly removed the sheet from Amin's face. Saeed and Abdol were standing next to him. When he saw the face, Saeed could not believe that it was actually Amin. But it was Amin. His face was swollen and dark blue with a darker swelling that covered a large area of his forehead up to the edge of his hair. The nose was broken and the upper lip torn apart, with a stream of dried blood dripping a thick dark line from his lips down to his neck and chin.

Saeed turned his head away and Abdol, with his knees shaking, moved toward the window. He stood there for a while and then returned to Hajji, who was bending over his son's body. The tears that Hajji had not been able to shed from the early morning suddenly began to cover his face, dripping onto his shoulders. Abdol led him toward the door. There, Majid, Hajji's driver took his other hand.

Saeed had not followed them. When Hajji left, he had knelt next to Amin and had burst into tears. Abdol, still assisting Hajji, looked back to see Amin's face, still illuminated by the ray of light through the window. This was the last time Abdol saw the face of his friend and childhood playmate.

●　　●　　●　　●　　●

I looked at Abdol's reddened eyes — those large black eyes that Amin used to describe as "the eyes of a frightened sheep."

"No tradition or custom can deny me the right to see my husband one last time," I said.

Abdol promised to let me see him once they washed and prepared the body for burial. Then I calmed down and asked where and how Amin was killed.

"It seems that he has been murdered," Soraya said softly.

"Who murdered him? The Revolutionary Guards?"

Abdol was quicker to respond to my question. "No. Right now, the Revolutionary Prosecutor and two of the ministers are with Hajji Agha. They believe that Amin was murdered by the Shah's secret police."

I turned my face toward Saeed who was leaning against the wall and looking at the garden through the window. I could not comprehend why former agents of the Shah's secret police would kill Amin.

"But why would they do such a thing?" I asked.

"They say that it is a kind of revenge for what Hajji has done for the Revolution," Abdol answered. "There have been similar cases."

"I have to talk to this prosecutor myself," I said.

I still do not know what I intended to tell him, but I needed to speak to someone who knew something about Amin's death. I was expected to sit and weep for my husband's death but, although I had already wept so furiously during the past week whenever I had thought about the possibility of his death, I could not now shed a tear. I did not even feel sad. In fact, I felt nothing. I was like someone curious to know about the death of a stranger she had not met.

Later on, Soraya told me, "You were not like people struck by a sudden shock. Not like those who lose a beloved person. You were not even like yourself. Your eyes were calm and there was no feeling in them. There was a ruthless chill in the way you talked and behaved toward us."

Soraya asked her husband to bring her briefcase from Esmat Khanum's room; once Abdol left, she asked me to lie down for a while. After that I was free to do whatever I wanted. I felt that she was treating me as if I had gone mad. When we were together in England I had once seen her talking to one of her patients, a young man who believed that God told him things of grave importance. But he did not know when God was going to talk to him next and therefore he refused to sleep. I was shocked to think that I, too, had gone mad.

"I'm all right, Soraya. Don't talk to me as if I'm one of your patients," I said.

"I know. There's nothing wrong with you," she laughed. "You behave quite normally. Why would I talk to you as a patient?"

Abdol returned with the briefcase. Saeed put his hand on my shoulder. "It's better if you rest for a while. We'll talk about everything later on."

Still sitting on the edge of the bed, I looked at Nargess. The sunlight was scattered on her face so that it resembled those features found on ancient gold Achæmenid coins.

"I'm not tired at all," I said.

Saeed pushed me down gently and made me stretch on the bed. Then he stood next to the bed and looked at me. Soraya came along with a syringe.

"This is to help you rest for a while, Luba," she said.

I felt a sense of relief. I felt that I needed some rest. Soraya took my arm and folded up my sleeve. I sensed the prick of the needle and soon everything began to fade away. Before falling asleep, I remembered my sons. I looked at Saeed, who was still standing next to the bed with his face seemingly superimposed on an ancient gold coin as big as the whole ceiling.

"I want to see my children," I said. And Saeed said something that I could not hear.

.6.

Amin was buried on August the twelfth with a lengthy ceremony. The Revolutionary Prosecutor supervised the investigation of the wreckage of Amin's car in Evin, in the northwest of Tehran. Soon afterward, the Revolutionary Council, in an official proclamation, recognized Amin as a martyr of the revolution and decided to bury him with all the honors saved for martyrs.

Amin's coffin was covered with the Iranian flag. The lion-and-sun emblem that had decorated the center of the flag during the Shah's regime was missing. The new regime had rejected the emblem and had not yet come up with a new one. The members of the Transitional Cabinet and the Revolutionary Council, together with the leaders of the Revolutionary Guards, all carrying big wreaths of flowers, accompanied the coffin to Emamzadeh Abdollah Cemetery, where Hajji's family tomb was located. Hajji and Bardia walked in the front row, shoulder to shoulder with government ministers and the Revolutionary Prosecutor. Bardia, who wore a black suit I had not seen before, looked like a young man. It was as if he had aged ten years in a matter of a few days. I was amazed by Bardia's dignified demeanor. Flanked by two Revolutionary Guards, he placed the wreath on the grave.

During the last forty-eight hours he had seen me only once. I had slept half of the time and I spent the other half either in Nargess's room or sitting next to her and Esmat Khanum, amid the ever increasing crowd of visitors. I had wanted to escape those obligatory social scenes. The collective wailing of the women, the maddening shrieks of Esmat Khanum and her sister, and the groans of Nargess had created an endless nightmare for me. No. It had a resting point. When the day and the fasting period came to an end, a few women stretched a long piece of cloth on the floor and set down various dishes of food. Women hastily began to eat and forced Esmat Khanum, her sister, and Nargess to join them for a few bites. Then the dishes were carried away and the piece of cloth was wrapped with the same haste. And immediately the inharmonious and intolerable symphony of moans and shrieks restarted. I was the center of attention during these rituals, but no one bothered to talk to me any more. Dressed in total black, with my hair under a black cover, I sat there with my heavy, sleepy eyes fixed on the red and azure flowers of the carpet, as I tried to escape the burden of those inquisitive looks on my skin.

Margaret and Soraya usually sat next to me. Soraya was always alert to whatever was going on around us. But Margaret was frightened by the constant commotion. Once, when I returned to Nargess's room, she followed me. There, she no longer seemed afraid. She could talk to Soraya in English, her native language. She asked Soraya a lot of questions about the Iranian customs regarding the death of a person. She wanted to know how long it could drag on. And Soraya, kind and gentle as always, answered her numerous questions and, all the while kept her eyes on me as well.

Bardia came to see me there in Nargess's room. His face was calm and pale. He took me in his arms and murmured into my ears, "Mama…," as if he wanted to say something more. But he remained silent. Before that, whenever I passed the room where the men sat with Hajji, I could see Bardia sitting amongst them with his head bowed. I was happy that he could sit with the men. In that room there was no shrieks and moaning. Men talked to each other in low voices and did not pay any attention to others, even to the reciter of the holy book, who sang the verses ceaselessly and untiringly with the large, loud speakers scattering his voice into every corner of the house.

Bahram mostly played in the garden with other children his age. He neither mixed with the men nor came into the room where the women were busy with their intangible chorus. If someone cared to call him when he passed by a room, he stopped for a moment and then, choked with unseen tears, retreated back to the garden. Once, I went to see him in the garden. He put his hands around my neck and looked at me with his worried eyes.

"Mama, I don't like crying. Don't cry."

"I am not crying, my dear."

"I don't like crying at all."

"Okay, dear. I won't cry."

On another occasion he asked, "Is Daddy going to come back?"

"No, dear."

Sedigheh Khanum, who was passing by, continued my sentence. "Your daddy has gone to where God is. He's in the sky."

"Is God very far from here?"

"Yes, very far."

"Sahand says he is dead."

"That's right. He is dead."

"Is he a God now?"

"No dear, good people go to where God is," Sedigheh Khanum corrected him.

● ● ● ● ●

The traditional mourning lasted for seven days. After the exhaustion of this period, I returned to my home. Soraya and Nargess had offered to come with me, but I had preferred to be left alone. I even welcomed the children's wishes to stay with their grandparents for a while. I needed some quiet. For eight days, the uninterrupted shrieks and the sorrowful voice of the reciter had filled my head with strange noises. I felt that I had lost my concentration forever.

It was in the tranquility of my home that Amin's face, which I had seen at the back of the mortuary before his burial, began to sink into my mind. They had brought him out of the mortuary in a simple wooden coffin. The coffin was covered with a hand-embroidered piece of cloth called *tagh-e shal*. Saeed and Soraya stood at my sides. The coffin was on a bench inside the hall, which led to the cemetery. Saeed gently pushed the *tagh-e shal* away and the inside of the coffin became visible. Amin was inside a white long sack called a *kafan*. Muslims put the naked body of the deceased inside it and bury the *kafan* without the coffin. The face of the deceased person is covered with a separate piece of *kafan*. Saeed pushed this piece aside and my eyes caught Amin's face. No. This was not his. I only could see a smashed nose and a torn lip scattered on a white and bluish background. It was as if I saw a mask. I did not even see the dark blue eyelid and the black swollen forehead that many others had noticed.

I sat in the armchair in which he used to sit every night, as his memory, alive and bright, lowered a curtain on everything that I had seen and heard during the last few days. Amin looked at me from the depths of our wedding picture on the small table next to the lamp. His large black eyes were shining and his opened lips formed the shape of a kiss. His hand was on my shoulder and I rested my head on his arm. A huge white lace covered my head and half of his shoulder. We had taken the photograph to show his family that we had married, a year earlier, with the proper ceremony.

I began to walk around the apartment. I found something of his everywhere I looked. His slippers were still in front of the bed. His pajamas rested untouched on the back of the chair. I could not move them. A black leather suitcase was still on the floor near the wardrobe. He had taken it out of the storage room so that I could prepare everything needed for a weekend trip I and the children were supposed to take to the north of Iran for the weekend. We had bought the suitcase eight years ago, when we were about to leave England for Iran.

As he was paying for it, Amin had told me, "This is the beginning of a new history in our lives."

From then on, he jokingly referred to the suitcase as "the beginning of history." Gradually it became a proper name for the black suitcase: "Let's take the History. It is much lighter." "Bring me the History." "The green suitcase is enough. We don't need the History one."

His toothbrush was in the brush holder and his razor was on the bathroom counter. *The History of French Revolution*, the last book he read, was still on his rocking chair. I picked up the book. There was a bookmark with a gilded picture of Big Ben between pages 114 and 115. I put the book back on the chair. On his desk there were a few neatly compiled books, along with those three letters Nargess had brought from Amin's office the night before his body was found. I opened the letters. The first one was an invitation from the British Gynecological Society for Amin to attend their annual conference. I thought that I should write and inform them that they should not expect him any more. The second letter was a thank-you card from John Taylor. He was returning Amin's best wishes on his birthday. I knew John. He was a colleague of Amin's when we were in London. The third letter seemed a little bit odd:

"Dear Amin. Your friends received the news and the gifts in good time. We are all thankful to you. Doctor sends you his best wishes. Rakhshan."

There was no date or address of the sender. Only the stamp on the envelope revealed that it had come from France. I thought Amin had, as usual, sent a present to a friend. But why "friends"? I left the letters on the desk and went into the kitchen.

I sat there looking at the panorama of Tehran, which was hardly visible in the afternoon sunlight and amid the suspended dusty air. Was I to remain in this city any more? Could I love this city as before?

I had fallen for Tehran during the first few weeks of my stay. Tehran was an ugly city at the foot of the beautiful Alborz Mountain range, with a huge mass of contrasting and haphazardly erected buildings, tall and short, old and modern, brick and cement, wide streets and narrow alleys. The main streets, with their modern buildings and colorful neon lights, were similar to many European roads, but the narrow alleys, though mostly made of patchy asphalt, seemed from the heart of the Middle Ages. Tehran was a city filled with crowds, cars, and ceaseless noise. It was a city which could madden any stranger during her first few days there. But, it could soon open its arms and embrace the visitors, warm and gentle as a mother's breast. One could not possibly remain a stranger in Tehran after a few weeks. Every eye is welcoming and appealing, whether it belongs to the poor, wandering peddlers who move around the city from early morning until late in the night, untiringly presenting their wares to the passing crowd; those arrogant wealthy men sitting behind the wheels of their expensive cars, who wait patiently in the ever-increasing traffic jams; the small shop owners who sell bread, vegetables, stationery, and kerosene all under the same roof; the boutique owners who exhibit the latest models of French, English, or Italian suits and dresses behind their windows; the lazy and restful passers-by who move along the pavement at nine o'clock in the morning as if in a park; or those of civil servants, who mostly engage in personal conversations and laughter rather than attend to their duties.

There was nothing in Iran which resembled my homeland but, from the very first weeks of my stay, I felt an old and familiar sense of tranquility and comfort of which I had been deprived from the early days of my childhood. Perhaps this feeling was due to the presence of Amin, his friends, and his family. Or it could have been because of a kind of welfare I had not experienced before.

I still loved that city. Even though Amin was not there anymore, I considered it home. I did not feel the same during my eight years in London. I did even have such sentiments for my birthplace. Here, both my children and I had an extended family. We had friends whom we had known for such a long time. I had a nice job, the likes of which I could not find in any other part of the world. And, above all, I was a citizen of Iran. I was an Iranian. Even if I wanted to go back to England I had no document other than a letter disclosing my status as a refugee before I left for Iran.

I could sell all of Amin's property, which was in both of our names. I could take the millions in cash we had in our shared bank account and leave with my children for England. This was an opportunity that did not arise for every woman after the revolution in Iran. New laws, ready for passage in the upcoming parliamentary session, denied women the right to be accepted as the guardians of their children. This guardianship, after the death of fathers, was handed over to the grandfathers. All of Amin's wealth, apart from this building, which he had bought in my name, would be owned by Hajji. But, just a few hours before I left his house, he had declared that all of the wealth, as well as the guardianship of the children belonged to me.

He had cast his heavily wrinkled eyes to the floor and had said, "You are our daughter. Don't ever think that by losing him anything has changed. You always have a place in our hearts. If you decide to stay in this country, you will give us much joy because you'll give us the chance to be with our grandchildren. They are the light of our lives. But if you decide to leave this country, you are free to do so, as well. You have the authority to sell everything you and Amin had and take your children away. In any event, we'll give you all the help you need."

Then he wiped the tears which were on the verge of disappearing into the lines around his eyes.

"I have never imposed anything on my children's lives. I will not impose anything on you or my grandchildren, either. Do whatever you think is necessary for your happiness."

Throughout those moments, and when I embraced him to kiss his wet face, I knew that I did not wish to leave Tehran. But was it right to think only of myself? What about the children? Although they had family and relatives in Iran, weren't they in serious danger because they were Amin's children? If he was murdered by those opposed to the revolution in an act of revenge, wasn't the shadow of this revenge lurking above my children's heads as well?

But there was something deep inside my soul that kept asking whether Amin truly was killed by the opponents of the new regime. What the government and the Revolutionary Prosecutor had told me had not satisfied this aspect of my thoughts. But who else could have killed him? Was he killed because of a personal enmity? Was his murder somehow related to that woman on whom Amin had performed an abortion? Were the people who had kidnapped Amin, and kept him for a week, and then brutally killed him somehow related to that woman? I was convinced that even if I was not to stay in Tehran for good, I would not leave the country before solving the mystery of Amin's disappearance and murder. And it was that very day, sitting in front of the hazy panorama of Tehran, when I made my mind to stay in Iran. When, on *Eid-e Fetr*, the festivity day at the end of the fasting month, I informed my husband's family about my decision, they were so ecstatic that I thought they had immediately forgotten half of the sorrows they had suffered because of Amin's death.

It was then that Saeed said, "Now that you are to remain in Iran, it would be better for you first to go to England with the children to rest for a short period."

Margaret was preparing for her own trip to England. She had planned to visit her family and invited me to her father's house in the suburbs of London. But I had no desire to go on such a trip. I needed to catch up on the work I had interrupted, as well as organize my children's lives.

.7.

I returned to work. September was coming to an end with a heat wave that, as I was told, was unparalleled in the last thirty years. It was a heat that one could feel melting the asphalt. It could penetrate the walls and enter air-conditioned rooms. September also brought some incredible events that put the Iranian people, who had just recently experienced the fervor of a grand scale revolution, face to face with some unforeseen and unfamiliar fears: independent newspapers were shut down one by one.

The same day Amin was buried, there was a huge demonstration in front of the Tehran University, protesting the closing of *Ayandegan*, an independent newspaper that had been taken over and run by the leftist activists after the revolution. It turned to be a futile protest. Then there were the Revolutionary Committee, which had begun the systematic slaughter of ordinary people in Sanandaj and Sardasht, two cities in the west of Iran. Civil servants were fired or tried by the hundreds under the pretext of "revolutionary cleansing." The remaining newspapers, which were mostly run under the supervision of the government, had daily lists of people who were being executed by the firing squads because of their connections with the previous regime. The heads of governmental offices were ordered to make sure all female civil servants were wearing their long uniforms and scarves. The new regulations which were supposed to become laws, clearly illustrated that the aim was to eliminate all of the rights and liberties for which the revolution had begun in the first place.

I was back in my office after two weeks of absence. The director of the Iran Archeological Museum was Yadollah Faramarzi, an elderly, amicable person who had taught archeology for years. Clearly depressed, he informed me that from then on I had to wear "suitable" dresses and scarves. Then there was another order: "They want us to gather all of the female sculptures and those pieces relating to the Zoroastrian religion and take them to the stockrooms."

While he was speaking, he was obviously trembling. After a pause, he said, "To be honest, I would rather this be done under your supervision. I am so worried about these pieces. This job should be done with extreme care and I know that you love them as much as I do."

The work began the next day. I was wearing a large scarf which slid down my shoulders every other minute, exposing my hair, so I repeatedly had to put it hastily back on my head. I had two assistants and it took us three weeks to handle the job. Every day we wrapped the images of the Sun — the ancient Iranian symbol of love and the final victory of virtue over vice — which had been engraved and carved on stone as well as gold and silver coins, in silicon paper and took them to the stockrooms in the basement of the museum, hiding them away without any signs of their tangible victory in their perpetual war against wickedness and evil. At the commencement of each new day, a new army of Anahita, the goddess of love, was discovered, diligent and uncompromising in another corner of the museum.

Some days I had to stay longer than the usual office hours and returned home exhausted late at night. The children were practically living in Hajji's place. After Amin's death they did not return but for a few short visits. Schools were out for the summer and I thought that they would be happier and safer in their grandparents' house. I, too, was more comfortable. I preferred to be left alone at home so I could have a drink and submerge into the sweet memories of my life with Amin.

Every other night, on my way home, I stopped at Hajji's house and spent a few hours with the children. Bahram scarcely asked about his father. He was totally absorbed by the toys that Hajji's family gave to him on almost a daily basis. But Bardia seemed to be deep in his thoughts. They had given him a separate room which had belonged to Amin before his departure for England. When I came over, Bardia came out of his room to see me. But his stay was short and he soon was back in his room. Others told me that he spent most of his time reading books. Whenever I asked him what he was reading, he mentioned the history of Islam. Once, I went into his room and saw him reading a book on Islam by Morteza Motahari. I later discovered that the writer was considered to be the major theoretician and the first martyr of the revolution.

Bardia's fascination with these religious books seemed rather strange to me. But I expected that once the schools reopened, he would return to his normal life. Nargess had the same opinion. One time, when I mentioned the books, she laughed.

"I had the same sentiments when I was his age," she said. "Amin was the same before going to England. He used to say his daily prayers and fast during Moharram. It seems that it is a Jalali syndrome. Every member of this family has to go through a phase of religious fervor. But they soon give it up."

These days Nargess was totally involved in what was being published by a group of Trotskyites. They were an active group of young people and Saeed was considered one of their leaders. Nargess did the paste-up work for the group's publications. Their activities took place in complete secrecy; I did not come to know about it until some time later. At that time, the leftist publications enjoyed the most popular readership. To those people who saw their power of protest fading away on a daily basis, the leftist approach to the leadership of the revolution seemed both attractive and plausible. Amongst the leftist groups, only the *Tudeh* Party was collaborating with the regime and, therefore, their publications were distributed without difficulty. This party was traditionally in line with the policies of the Soviet Union and, accordingly, there was an ongoing clash between them and the other leftists who were differentiated from them as "Independents."

These clashes had affected our small group of friends, as well. Abdol, who suddenly joined the Tudeh Party after the revolution, constantly was the target of attacks by Saeed and Nargess. Even his wife Soraya, who used to try her best not to get involved in political discussions, did not approve of her husband's politics. Saeed even went so far as to sever his relations with Abdol, whom he had been friends with for a long time. Amin's disappearance and death brought about a short period of cease-fire between them. But soon, particularly after the massacre of Kurdish people in Sanandaj, the silence of the Tudeh Party, as well as its alignment with the regime, initiated a new period of war between the old friends. Saeed, Nargess, and their "comrades" could not understand how the so-called "Children of Lenin" could make a truce with a reactionary, religious, and brutal regime.

There was also the Mojahedin Organization, a religious leftist group that had been labeled as "Islamic Marxists" by the Shah's regime long before the advent of the revolution. For months after the revolution, the organization was united with the new regime on many fronts, but, later, it began to separate itself from it and take critical positions. The first instance of this separation came when the government ordered them to surrender the weapons they had gathered during the revolution. The next incident was the sudden death of Ayatollah Taleghani, one of the most important and popular leaders of the revolution, who openly supported the Mojahedin Organization. The cause of his death was announced as a heart attack, but supporters of Mojahedin, if not the organization itself, believed he was murdered by the collaborators of the new regime. Nevertheless, this was not publicly announced by their organization.

● ● ● ● ●

After someone dies, there is traditionally a gathering of relatives and friends on the fortieth night in Iran. They call it *chelleh* (meaning the fortieth day). The *chelleh* for Amin brought us together once again but in a totally different atmosphere. The participants were deeply immersed in current political discussions mostly centered on the clashes between the regime, the Mojahedin, and the leftist groups. There was also a piece of news about the execution of twenty-five alleged collaborators with Shahpour Bakhtiar, the last prime minister of the Shah, who was then in Paris, leading an opposition group against the new regime. But it did not attract major attention during the gathering. In truth, apart from the occasional groans of Esmat Khanum, one could hardly find any references to Amin. It was a political meeting rather than a memorial gathering.

While others were momentarily talking about Bakhtiar, Soraya told me that she had seen the name of Dr. Jahangiri on a list of Bakhtiar's collaborators.

"He's so lucky to be in Paris," she said. "If they could get their hands on him, he'd surely be dead by now."

I knew Dr. Jahangiri and his wife, Mahshid, from my days in London. They were Amin's friends when the three were active in the Confederation of Iranian Students outside the country. But when I came to know them again some years later, they had given up all political activities. They had come to Iran a year after us. We saw each other in Tehran only about once every two or three months, and each time for some formal occasion. Amin was working in the same hospital as Dr. Jahangiri; it was usually through him that I sometimes heard about them. A few days before they left Iran, Mahshid telephoned me to say farewell and said that they were going to London for a month.

"But Mahshid told me that they were going to London," I told Soraya.

"Definitely to mislead you," Abdol, who had been listening, answered. "They have now been in Paris for quite some time. I saw his name in the last announcement published by Bakhtiar's group."

I do not recall how I suddenly remembered the letter anonymously sent to Amin from Paris. I tried to recall its details. I could not do so, but a sudden rush of anguish was overcoming me. It was because of this unexpected feeling that, at the end of the gathering, I asked Saeed to see me home. I wanted to tell him about the letter. He was the closest and most reliable person I knew then.

I had scarcely seen Saeed during the last month. He was not in a good mood. Margaret had filed for divorce as soon as she had reached England. She had sent him a copy of the petition, which included application for the guardianship of their daughter, Lili. It was clear that Margaret had made her mind up before leaving Iran. Years later she told me that she had kept her decision a secret while she was in Iran because she was afraid that Saeed or his family would not let her to return to England with Lili. Nevertheless, and contrary to his family's wishes, Saeed had sent his acceptance as soon as he received Margaret's letter.

"My mother cries day and night for Lili," he once told me. "She blames me for giving her to Margaret. But what else could I do? Even if we were in England the court would give her to her mother. And why should I take the child away from her mother? I have no clear and established life here. My life is suspended in the air."

Nosrat Khanum, his mother, was undoubtedly happy that Margaret had left his son. She had not liked her daughter-in-law from the beginning. Nargess believed the mother simply could not like any other woman in her son's life. Unlike her sister, who had given Amin his independence, Nosrat Khanum considered Saeed an inseparable part of her own existence and, like so many Iranian mothers-in-law, preferred her son to marry a woman of her choosing. At the same time, she believed that Lili belonged to her and Saeed. This belief was the basis of her frequent accusations, which usually resulted in bitter confrontations between mother and son.

Saeed was not in a good mood. I asked him what was wrong.

"They have bombarded Paveh in Kurdistan," he said.

"Do you have any friends there?"

"They are all our friends." There was a bitter reproach in his voice.

I decided not to talk about the letter and postpone it for a better time. But his voice was softer when he said, "I'm sorry, Luba. I don't feel well at all. What a good idea to invite me to accompany you home. How are you?"

"Saeed, I wanted to talk to you about something. I wonder if you have the time or you're in the mood for it," I said after a short pause.

"Sure. Why not? I always have the time and mood for you."

At home, I poured two drinks for ourselves and, after taking the first sip, began to tell Saeed about the letter.

"Tonight Soraya told me that she has seen Dr. Jahangiri's name in newspapers. They say he has been a spy for the CIA and Bakhtiar. Do you think that there is any truth to that?"

Saeed, clearly feeling much better, smiled. "Yes. I know that he is in Paris and collaborates with Bakhtiar."

I went to the other room and brought the letter: "Do you remember this? You and Nargess brought it from Amin's office the night before his body was found. It seems a little odd to me. I don't recognize the sender."

Saeed read the letter. Without looking at me, he said, "Dr. Jahangiri was known as Rakhshan when he was active in the Confederation."

I took the letter back and read it again. The internal anguish had returned.

"I don't understand this. He is talking about news and gifts. What kind of news and gifts could Amin send for Jahangiri's friends? And why he is writing this letter under that name?"

Saeed lit a cigarette and looked at me with his bright brownish eyes.

"Luba, I did not intend to tell you this. I know that Amin had some connection with Bakhtiar and his followers. He most probably was killed because of this association."

He did not let me stop him. It was as if he wanted to tell me everything as fast as he could in order to release himself from the burden of such a grave secret. He told me that one of his friends was arrested for a week. While he was being interrogated, he had seen Amin strapped in a chair, with his face broken and bleeding, on the same day that we were in the morgue. Saeed's friend had seen some Revolutionary Guards asking Amin different questions and had overheard someone mention Bakhtiar's name.

I was completely shocked. "Are you sure that the man he saw was Amin?"

"Definitely. He had met Amin twice in my house before. Besides, we have received news from other sources as well. Amin was killed by the guards because of his relation with Bakhtiar."

A huge rush of anger suddenly poured into my head and heart. I felt my face becoming warm and red. My body began to shake and my voice was harsh and trembling.

"And why did you remain silent? Why didn't you tell me these things? Why didn't you tell Hajji? Why didn't you write it in your newspaper? Why? Because he was not one of your comrades?"

Every word made me more angry and spread a rush of pain over my entire body. I was sure that the shaking in my body was clearly detectable. Saeed stood up and came toward me.

"Calm down, Luba, calm down. We could not possibly announce this. We had no documentation verifying our claims and no one would have paid any attention to us. Even if people would believe us, it was not a sound thing to do. We would have achieved nothing but the endangerment of other people's lives. Even you and your children could have been affected. You could not remain in this country. Everybody would look at you and the children as anti-revolutionary elements. Do you understand the meaning of a charge such as collaborating with America and Bakhtiar?"

Silence prevailed for a few seconds. Then Saeed continued, this time slowly and decidedly, looking at me to evaluate the impact of each word.

"Nargess advised this decision. She was the one who reminded us about the potential dangers for you and your children."

As he spoke, my anger began to turn into a deep dread. It was an old, forgotten fear that returned to me anew. I could see that the passage of twenty one years had not erased it at all. I could vividly remember that upon the arrest of my mother and her friends, others were determined to avoid us. The fear of being rejected had not left me at all.

Saeed took a tissue out of the box and handed it over to me. I wiped my eyes.

"But if they have arrested and killed Amin, why haven't they announced it?'

"We don't have a coherent government in this country. The power is scattered between different groups. We have the cabinet, the clergy, the Imam, and his household, and so on. Every group has a share in the power. We are sure that the transitional government of Bazargan has had no role in Amin's case. The guards have killed him on their own. Of course, even if the government was aware of what was happening, it could not prevent it. It is due to this fortunate — or perhaps unfortunate — fact that they have not announced what they have done to Amin. There is another aspect to it as well. No side would benefit from pushing Hajji towards the opposition. Until now, this revolution has been operational because of the money donated by Hajji and others.

"Even now, the real power keeping this regime alive belongs to people like Hajji, who enjoy a tremendous spiritual and material position in this society. If Hajji was aware that his son was murdered by these people he not only would not carry on supporting the regime, but the whole traditional trade sector of the country would side against them. Hajji and his friends hold the real power in Bazaar; it is this power that could break the backbone of the Shah's regime. At the moment, Bazaar supports the new regime. Even Bakhtiar and his friends, who come from traditional nationalist and Bazaari backgrounds, would not benefit from such a disclosure. Hajji is a nationalist to the depth of his bones. There are many others like him in the government. None of these parties would benefit from alienating Bazaaris at this stage. Bakhtiar counts on friends who are very near to the regime. His followers can penetrate into the power structure through this network of connections and wait for the right moment."

His voice echoed in my head like a faraway and unfamiliar murmur. It took me a while to gather myself together and say a few hollow words when he fell silent.

"If Hajji and his friends are so powerful, then they can stop these people."

Saeed chuckled and continued. "Although the disclosure of Amin's case is not desirable for all these factions, they are ready to clamp down on any kind of resistance should the very existence of the regime be on the line. Just look at the Kurdistan issue. A few months ago, they tried to solve the problem in a non-confrontational manner. When their tactics were unsuccessful, the Imam issued the order for the massacre of the Kurdish people...."

I interrupted him. "Sorry, Saeed. But I cannot believe that Amin, who hated the Shah's regime so much, could collaborate with his last prime minister. He always considered himself a supporter of the National Front and Dr. Mossadegh."

"The National Front was not against the Shah. It adhered to the constitutional monarchy but believed that the King should not interfere in the affairs of the state. They wanted to limit the powers of the Shah. Mossadegh himself propagated this. Thus, although Amin was against the Shah, he actually opposed a Shah who had broken the provisions of the Constitution. He was not against the institution of monarchy. In addition, after Mossadegh, the National Front was divided into two camps. The schism was between the religious elements and the modernist ones. Bazargan and his followers sided with the religious clergy and they are now a part of the new regime, whereas others, such as Bakhtiar, remained faithful to the old Constitution. When Amin saw that the new regime was not what he had expected, he chose to support the other section of the National Front."

Saeed tried to explain everything convincingly. I noticed that when he was talking about Amin, he did not show the compassion of a cousin who had lost an old friend. This made me resist what he was saying. I also had not yet received an answer.

"But what kind of help could Amin give them?'

Saeed smiled bitterly and was quick to answer back. "Dr. Jahangiri's letter clearly provides you with an answer. He could give them inside information which he could get through Hajji and his friends without arousing any suspicion. And also money."

The first part of what he said was feasible. But Amin could not have helped them financially without my knowledge. I was aware of all of his financial affairs, including his income from the office and the rent from the apartments, which were mostly cash and had been regularly handed over to me. There was no significant income from other sources. These funds were only enough to provide him with pocket money. He also had some income from his surgical operations and obstetric works which was debited to our shared account.

I looked up and stared in Saeed's eyes with confidence. "But I know everything about Amin's financial affairs. He couldn't possibly pay a large sum of money to anybody without me knowing it."

"Couldn't he have a separate account for himself?"

"He had one. But his main income was debited to our shared account. There is still a handsome sum in that account. The only large amounts of money in his hands related to the sale of the lower floors of his office. We intended to use that money to buy a house in Shemiran."

"When did he sell those lower floors?" Saeed asked with amazement.

"A month before his disappearance."

"And where is the money?'

"In his personal account."

"Do you know how much it was?"

"Six million, eight thousand Tomans."

"And are you sure that the money is still in that account?"

"Of course I'm sure. If he had wanted to touch the money, he would have informed me. He never hid anything from me."

I could hear my voice filled with a sense of pride. But I noticed that a bitter smile appeared on Saeed's lips for a fraction of a second. I felt that it was scornful.

"Am I right to say that you don't believe me?" I asked.

Then I stood up and, while going to the other room, added, "He always kept his checkbook at home."

I went to Amin's desk. He usually kept his important documents in its drawers. The first drawer was for the documents relevant to the buildings. He kept our marriage certificate and children's identity cards in the second. The third drawer was for the children's bank accounts. He usually kept his checkbook in this drawer as well. I had seen him putting it there when he had sold the lower floors and deposited the money into his personal bank account.

When I returned to the living room, Saeed was standing in front of the large painting on the wall, staring at it with full attention. It was as if he were seeing it for the first time. The painting showed a horse with a woman's head. Half of the woman's face was filled with joy and laughter but the other side was covered with sorrow and pain. Ahmad had painted it. I had bought it at the first exhibition I had seen of his work.

"The checkbook is not here," I said in a low voice. "He definitely forgot to bring it home after he deposited the money. It should be in his desk drawer at the office."

I did not believe what I was saying. Amin was very immaculate in keeping all his documents organized. I could hardly remember him taking something and not returning it to its place afterwards.

"Sure. It should be in the office," Saeed said. His voice seemed hollow and artificial.

I felt that there were some other things that he knew but was reluctant to tell me.

• • • • •

Saeed never talked about Amin; in fact, he hadn't said a word about Amin since I married him. Before I met Amin, Saeed used to talk about him a lot. It was perhaps because of Saeed's comments that when I first met Amin I felt that I had known him for years. But there was a difference between what I saw and what I had heard. I found Amin to be much more amicable than Saeed had described. In those days, I believed that Saeed had mixed feelings for him — a mixture of love and hate.

Saeed was five years younger than Amin. His mother, Nosrat Khanum, had chosen Amin as an ideal model for her son since his early childhood. The way Amin behaved, walked, talked, and attended to his lessons were to be copied by her young son. Under such pressure, Saeed had tried for fifteen years to copy someone whom he did not like. He detested the way Amin appeared, the way he talked, his calmness and indifference, and even the way he attended to his studies. He would sense a pretension and flashiness about Amin and believed that his behavior was always aimed at gaining admiration from others. He believed there was no naturalness or spontaneity about Amin. He did not even approve of Amin's appearance, which others found quite attractive. He considered Amin's appearance to be a source for his selfishness and baseless pride.

When Amin went to England at age twenty, Saeed was relieved for a while. But this relief did not last long. Despite the fact that the financial situation of Saeed's family was not comparable to that of Hajji's, Nosrat Khanum decided to force her son to go to England before he finished high school in Iran. Saeed's father was against this decision but did not have the authority to resist Nosrat Khanum. Amin was in England to study medicine and Saeed was to follow in his steps.

Saeed, who initially hated England, soon realized that once out of the reach of his mother's hands, he had the opportunity to rebel against her. When he was prepared to enter the university, he wrote to his family and announced that he wanted to become an architect rather than a medical practitioner. Nosrat Khanum was furious, but neither her letters nor her telephone calls could change Saeed's decision. His mother was so angry that she did not contact him for a year and stopped her financial support. He was forced to work to earn his living and to pay his university expenses. There was, of course, some occasional secretive money from his father. Colonel Shams had no will power vis-a-vis his wife, but one could always sense the potential for a sudden uprising against Nosrat Khanum within him. At the end of the first year Nosrat Khanum surrendered and, by forgiving her son, squashed the possibility of that potential eruption in her husband.

Although Saeed had released himself from his mother's influence, there was still that penetrating and ever-present influence of Amin overshadowing his life. Amin behaved like a big brother to him, an older and wiser brother who did not need a lot of force to impose his will on Saeed. He always kept an eye on Saeed, introduced him to his friends, insistently invited him to his numerous parties and praised him effusively at such gatherings. Amin never asked him why he had decided not to study medicine, but he had repeatedly named other universities at which Saeed could get better training as an architect. It was at Amin's place that Saeed met his first serious girlfriend in England. Amin had introduced them to each other and had spoken so highly of Saeed that the young girl had fallen for him immediately. On the surface, Saeed listened to Amin and accepted whatever he said, but sometimes, consciously or subconsciously, he tried to defy Amin's opinions and tastes. He consciously did not transfer universities and found an excuse to sever his relations with his girlfriend, whom he liked a lot. He felt that he could not possibly love a woman who was, as he put it, "selected by Amin."

Then he began to distance himself from Amin even further. He scarcely went to visit him and did not attend Amin's parties. He tried hard not to appear in places where Amin might be present. This led to a long period of total disconnection. It was during this very period that he became interested in political issues, particularly socialist viewpoints, and came to know new people whom he used to call "my leftist comrades." Once, upon an invitation from one of them, he attended a general meeting held by the Confederation of Iranian Students. During this meeting, he confronted Amin after a long period of separation. The confederation was an organization for different political creeds; Saeed soon realized that Amin was active in the National Front faction of the Confederation. During that meeting, they became engaged in a hot political debate. Amin, for the first time, lost his temper and angrily protested against Saeed's assertions. Saeed suddenly felt that Amin was not talking to him as an older and wiser brother anymore. This helped him to see that Amin's shadow was no longer present in his life.

Then Saeed realized that he actually liked Amin very much. He began to appear at Amin's parties once again, this time by his own will and not because of his family connections with Amin. Saeed was not much of a partygoer, but he willingly attended Amin's parties for the occasion to debate political issues with his cousin in peace. It seemed that there was no single issue upon which they could come to an agreement.

It was during those days that I came to know Saeed. Although I used to see him every day, I did not meet Amin for the next seven months. Saeed tried twice to take me to Amin's parties and I refused to go. I was in a very bad mood in those days. My separation from Milan, my father's death, my homesickness for my own distant country, and my thoughts about the child I had inside me had consumed all my energy and enthusiasm to go out and meet new people.

I considered Saeed my only friend. I have always thought that if I had not met him during the very first days I was in England and had he not insisted on being with me, my days would have been hellish. I was a total stranger in England; I knew no one and nowhere. The only thing I had done was register for a language class at London University. A few days after the class had begun, I was paying for my food at the college cafeteria when I met Saeed. I had not yet mastered British currency and was wondering which bills to hand over to the cashier. Saeed was behind me in line. He bent over, took one of the notes, and handed it over to the cashier. I thanked him and he followed me to a table.

As soon as he sat down, I heard him say, "Would you believe me if I told you that I have never seen a girl as beautiful as you?"

His face immediately turned red, as if the words had jumped out of his mouth without his control. From then on, he appeared daily with his food tray at my table. But he never complimented me again. Although I had studied the English language in Czechoslovakia, speaking English was not easy for me. Saeed, despite the impatience I had sensed in him, listened to me with rapt attention and corrected my sentences.

Soon I told him all about myself and we became close friends who spent most of our time together. Every day, he taught me something new that brought another ray of color to my life. Although he was only three years older than me, he seemed a lot more experienced and knowledgeable. But this sophistication hid behind layers of shyness and innocence. I think if he had not this diffidence, Amin never could have taken me away from him. I did not even know how deep he had fallen in love with me in those days.

Saeed himself introduced me to Amin. I was eight months pregnant when I suffered a sudden unbearable pain. Saeed was horrified and took me to a hospital where he knew Amin was working as a resident. Two months later, when I telephoned him to say that Amin and I were getting married, he paused for a long time and then, in broken words, said, "So tell him to invite me, too." Although he didn't usually play jokes, I didn't interpret his words as anything other than a light humor.

He disappeared for two weeks and after that he seldom came to see me. From then on we met each other as relatives rather than friends. Once or twice, when I had some quarrels with Amin, I went to see him. He listened to me but did not say anything about Amin. At the end of such meetings he would say, "These are not important issues. You can easily resolve them. The important thing is that you love each other."

•　•　•　•　•

The day after my discussion with Saeed, I finished my work at the office earlier than usual and went to Amin's office. I opened the front door and, before going in, removed a small note on the door that read, "The office is closed until further notice." Abdol had put up the note two days after Amin's disappearance. I climbed the well-cleaned stairs that led to the waiting room. My heart beat hard, like a broken drum. As I ascended the stairs I felt that I missed Amin more and more. It was not dark yet but I switched on the lights. Everything was untouched — the two small sofas with wooden handles, a short, square table with a pile of neatly organized magazines, and a desk near the entrance, where Soudabeh used to sit.

Amin and I had bought that desk three years before, when the number of patients had begun to rise. Amin had hired Soudabeh after putting a small advertisement in the evening papers. He had said, "It didn't take me more than two minutes to hire her. She is not bad at all. She needs the job; she's not taking it just to kill time." But the interview had taken ages for Soudabeh. It had taken so long that Soudabeh had never forgotten it.

The office was closed for lunch. Dr. Jalali sat on a sofa in the waiting room and leafed through a foreign magazine. He raised his head when he heard Soudabeh say hello. Soudabeh thought the man was very attractive. When Amin stood up to shake hands with her, Soudabeh felt shy because of her height. She could hardly reach the doctor's shoulders. Contrary to what Soudabeh had expected, the doctor did not bombard her with numerous questions. He talked about general things and only once, amid other things, did he ask her why she was looking for a job in a doctor's office. The way he talked helped to subside Soudabeh's anxiety. She felt that even if she did not get the job she would be happy to sit there and talk to Dr. Jalali. His friendliness had given her enough courage to admit that she was not specifically looking for a job in a doctor's office.

"I need to work. I need the money," she said. "This is my sixth interview. The other five did not employ me...."

Dr. Jalali interrupted her. "The sixth one accepts you, on one condition...."

And before Dr. Jalali could name his condition, Soudabeh said, "I accept it. Whatever it is."

From the beginning of the next week, Soudabeh worked behind the desk we had bought only the day before.

Apart from a telephone, a glass containing a few pens, and two black-and-blue notebooks, there were no other items on Soudabeh's desk. I passed through the narrow hall and entered the office. The whiteness of the walls and the operating table almost blinded me. It was as if I was looking at that expanse of whiteness for the first time. Amin's chair, empty and lonely, was behind his desk. I could not sit in it. I remained standing in front of the desk and gazed at its surface. There was that little signet frame, with a photograph taken of the children and me when Bahram was a year old and Bardia was nine. Amin had taken the photo himself, on a sunny spring day at the foot of the Damavand mountains amid the wild bushes of fresh red poppies. We were standing amid the flowers and smiling at Amin. I took the frame and put it in my purse. Then I went around the desk and opened the first drawer. I noticed that my fingers were trembling. There was nothing but a few blank prescription notes. It was in the second drawer that I found his check book amongst a pile of letters and notes.

I discovered the truth then and there. In July, one month before his death, Amin had withdrawn four million and two thousand Tomans from his personal account in three installments. On each of the three check stubs he had written "Cash for Rakhshan." It was his writing. I realized, without a doubt, that my late husband had helped Bakhtiar. But how on earth could he have done so? If he was alive and we were going to buy the house, how could he have explained this to me?

I felt ashamed for being so confident when I talked to Saeed about Amin's attitude toward financial matters. I felt so humiliated. It was not the absence of money that bothered me. It was Amin's secretiveness that hurt me so much.

• • • • •

That night I told Nargess and Saeed, whom I had invited to my place, what had happened. Nargess shrugged and said, "Amin is a different person to me now. His death has destroyed so many things in me. You shouldn't think about these matters anymore, either. Don't tell this story about the money to anyone. Even to my father. Disclosing Amin's relations with Bakhtiar would result in nothing but danger for everyone."

The indifference in her voice was totally new to me. I thought that her gradual absorption into the political organization had created her attitude. She judged everything from her political point of view, even when she was talking about the death of a brother whom she so dearly loved. I was familiar with this kind of attitude from my early youth and felt that I could understand why she was talking in that manner. Amin now belonged to a political faction whose ideology was totally opposed to that of Nargess and her friends. This difference was strong enough to wash away all emotions. Perhaps it was because of this interpretation that later on, when I came to know other hidden facts, I felt so ashamed and my affection for her was greatly altered. But that night, I was very annoyed by her words.

"You shouldn't be bothered by Amin's secretiveness, either," Saeed said. "There are so many men who prefer not to talk about their political activities with their wives."

This could not heal my wounded soul, as my resentment deepened with each passing day. Before I knew about Amin's political activities, I had considered his murderers to be the cause of all of my troubles. But now, I felt that Amin was even more responsible than those who had killed him.

Upon his death, my only joy was to spend my nights reliving the past, memories that I seldom recalled when Amin was alive. Even if I could recall them, the pictures were not sharp enough to absorb me for a long time. But after his death they gradually became so sharp that I could enjoy every one of them. I was like a little girl suddenly discovering the joys of adolescence and experiencing the mix of pain and pleasure, as she thinks about an unattainable lover. I was becoming addicted to reliving memories of Amin. It is only now that I realize the fictional nature of many of my pleasing thoughts which I had previously considered to be accurate portrayals. From myself and Amin, I had created a couple of lovers who flew in the sky, addicted to each other's presence. I flew with him. I made love to him. I told him so many things that I had never said or felt inclined to say during our real married life. But my dreams always had only one ending: his death. I would jump up, alarmed and confused as if I had just then received the bad news. The only way out of this dead end was alcohol or tranquilizers.

But the new information about his political activities wrapped all of those sweet dreams in a blanket of clouds. I became alerted and inquisitive, always searching for other clues to his secretive activities. On Wednesdays he would attend meetings at the hospital and would come home two hours later than usual. Could he have gone to other meetings in those two hours? Every day at lunchtime, he said he dined at a small restaurant opposite his office. Could this have been an excuse to go somewhere else? Sometimes he had long and difficult operations. Could they have been made up to cover the truth? Then I remembered that one Wednesday Bahram was ill and I called Amin at the hospital. He was in a meeting with other doctors. I remembered that a few times I had gone to his office at lunchtime without prior notice and had found him in the small restaurant opposite his place of work as he ate his food in solitude. But if he saw people at the office…? What if…? And I could never come to a solid conclusion. Then I had to resort to alcohol and tranquilizers to put myself to sleep. Soraya, who had prescribed the pills during the first week of Amin's death, had warned me to stop taking them. But I could not help it. I increased the number of tablets.

.8.

When the schools reopened, I brought the children back home. From the very first week, I noticed how they had changed. Bahram had become very sensitive and spoiled; and every little resistance to his wishes caused him to cry for a long time. Because I did not know how Esmat Khanum and Sedigheh managed to calm him, it took me a lot of time and effort to please him. Bardia had turned silent and aggressive. He did not pay any attention to other children and their games. The energetic young boy of a few months ago was replaced by a young man who, on returning from school, went directly to his room and gazed out of the window. He did not let Bahram or me go into his room. His only joy was at school. He attended his classes with sheer devotion. On the first day at school, they had introduced him as the son of a martyr to other boys and he was appointed the leader of his class.

Before the revolution, his school was private and mixed. By confiscating the private schools after the revolution, the education ministry had taken over his school as well. They had halved the building by erecting a long wall and had separated the boys from the girls. The previous head of the school had been an experienced and educated woman. In time for the reopening of the school at the beginning of the new academic year, however, Najafabadi, a less qualified man, was appointed as the headmaster. He had spent a few years in the Shah's prison with Ayatollah Montazeri, one of the leaders of the revolution.

I met Najafabadi a month after the school was opened. Bardia, joyful and delighted, had informed me that he would not be coming home for lunch from that day on. The reason was that he had become the leader of prayers at the school mosque—a room which was allocated for religious rites. I was furious, But Bardia, in an aggressive mood, told me that the matter was decided by the headmaster. Those days I did not come home for lunch, but Fatemeh Khanum, the elderly maid who worked at our apartment from seven thirty in the morning until five in the evening, would pick up the children from school, give them their lunches, and return them back to school. The schools were closed between noon and two in the afternoon; I did not want my children to stay at school during this time.

Before I uttered a word, Najafabadi began to tell me stories about his political activities, and the time he had spent in prison, and the kind of torture to which he had been exposed. Then he spoke of his admiration for Bardia. It was a difficult job to stop him to explain that I did not want Bardia to stay at school during lunch. He was clearly annoyed.

"But I am not sort of the man who goes back on his word. If you wish otherwise, you have to convince him yourself. But I think you should be proud that your son has been selected as the leader of the prayers."

I soon realized that he not only would not help me, but he was also quite capable of encouraging Bardia to confront me. I decided not to say anything more, even to Bardia. Before bringing the children home from Hajji's place, Soraya had warned me about the urgency of taking the children back. She believed Amin's death had confused Bardia and he was recreating Amin inside himself. But this invisible Amin had the attributes of a hero created by Bardia's subconscious wishes. This hero was martyred because of his beliefs. He was the representative of God on earth and had come to guide people to their salvation. Soraya told me that Bardia thought he should finish the mission his father had left incomplete.

I could understand that Amin's death would have a deep impact on Bardia and I regarded the change as a natural process. I myself had gone through the same process when I had lost my mother, and I had been two years older than Bardia when that incident happened. On the other hand, I could not forget that Bardia was going through adolescence and all of his moods and attitudes could be temporary.

Soraya accepted this last point and said, "It is on these important grounds that you should take him back home." She believed that any impact of Amin's death on Hajji and his wife, who were already very religious and could develop a sense of vengeance, could be considered as natural. But such attitudes in a young boy were intoxicating and dangerous.

So I was very glad that my children returned home after the summer holidays. But the new situation was neither to their nor their grandparents' satisfaction. The couple did not say anything specific, but Esmat Khanum telephoned to chat with the children every night. To keep them all happy, I agreed to take the children to stay with their grandparents during the Iranian weekends, which began Thursday afternoons and ended Friday nights. Every Thursday, Hajji's driver took the children directly from school to Hajji's house; on Friday evenings I went to see Hajji and Esmat Khanum and pick up the children.

This arrangement resulted in my being left alone during the weekends. Before Amin's death, Soraya and I would frequent a tennis club where I was a member every Thursday afternoon. As a result of the revolution, tennis clubs were either closed or segregated. Nevertheless, we had been able to find a tennis club for women. We would go to this club and play for two hours before having lunch together. But like my other hobbies, I gave up this activity after Amin's death.

• • • • •

On the last Thursday in October, I returned home from work to find Nargess in my apartment. She was sitting in the kitchen and Fatemeh Khanum was setting the table. She seemed to be in a good mood. It was the first time I had seen her so happy since her brother's death. In the past few months, she had lost some weight and her bright, black eyes were covered with a mist. But that day I noticed that her eyes had regained their youthful life and naughtiness. She was like a patient who had weathered a serious illness and was on the course of certain recovery.

She put her arms around me and kissed me. I sensed that she wanted a favor. I was right. She had come to convince me to go with her for a few days to Golsara in the North of Iran, on the edge of the Caspian Sea. Golsara was the name of a mansion that Hajji had inherited from his father. Amin was not fond of the place but I loved it. Since the early days of our stay in Iran, I had gone there often with Nargess and our other friends. But during the last few months, I had not even thought about the place. Nargess would go there more than anyone else and often said she would like to live there permanently.

But I was sure that she was not the sort of woman who could settle down in such a rustic atmosphere.

I reminded Nargess that I could not possibly interrupt the children's schedules. If they were to stay in Hajji's house longer than just for the weekends, they soon would realize that they could live there for the rest of the week, as well. Her persistence, which usually was successful, could not change my mind. At last she finally gave up.

Then, while watching Fatemeh Khanum, who was busy with her job, Nargess addressed me softly. "Someone is coming with me whom you like very much and I'm sure you'll be happy for me if I tell you that I'm falling in love with him."

I don't know why, but I immediately thought she was talking about Saeed. Although Nargess had finally found someone who could be a suitable friend for her as well, I did not feel happy at all. I did not understand my feelings at that moment, but I remembered that I had not been glad when I was told that Saeed was going to marry Margaret. But I pretended to be caught by a joyful surprise.

"So there is some good news amid the bad," I said.

Nargess stood up. "Let's go into another room. I cannot bear being in the kitchen for more than an hour," she said.

Throughout the seven years that I had known Nargess, she had never been with a man of her own. I knew that there were many men who had their eyes on her, but it seemed to me that she was reluctant to open up her world to any man. She had been separated from her husband for just a few months before we came to Iran. She had fallen in love with and married him during her first year at the university. Her parents were against both her marriage and her divorce. From the very first day, they had said that the man was not suitable for her. But once they had accepted their daughter's marriage, they preferred her to continue living with her husband despite the difficulties. "Men are like this. They'll be tamed after a few years," Esmat Khanum would say. Although Nargess had argued with her parents for a few months to make them accept her marriage, once she had made up her mind to divorce, she had not paid any attention to the protests of her parents and her husband. This attitude was quite rare for an Iranian woman.

During my years in Iran, I had noticed that most of the Iranian women — even those who had higher education — did not consider their husband's infidelity a good reason for divorce. I had heard many of them say, "Men are all like that," or "Remember, he is a man!" But Nargess had told me on several occasions that she would rather live alone than marry a man who assumed certain rights for himself because he was a man. "I want to find a man like Amin," she usually added with a smile.

Actually, Amin was everything to her. She loved him more than her parents. Her attitude toward him was the affection of a daughter for her father. A gap of fourteen years between the siblings had created a certain aura about Amin in her mind. She looked up to Amin and accepted whatever he said. She was only six years old when Amin left Iran to begin his studies in England and, during the next sixteen years, she had waited for him patiently. She was happy with the old pictures and memories she had of her brother. Every now and then, a short letter from Amin added to this happiness. Once in high school, she had persistently asked her father to send her to England for her university education. She knew that Amin was unable to return to Iran because of his political activities in the Confederation.

Amin had repeatedly wrote her, "I wish I could come back to Iran and see you all. But I do not want to take the risk of coming and then being unable to return here to finish my studies." Just when Nargess was studying for her final examination at school, Amin informed her that we would be coming to Iran shortly, although it took us three more years to do so. During this period, Nargess did not show any interest in going to England. She preferred to stay in Iran and attend her university there. So she had gone to Tehran University, married, and waited for Amin to come home.

After we settled in Iran, Nargess came to visit on a daily basis. She sought her brother's opinions on everything and almost always followed his advice. She spent most nights at our place, as well. She had her own key and was considered a permanent member of the family. Then came the period of popular uprisings. It was as if Iranians had suddenly awakened to remember that they had an appointment with history. We saw less of Nargess in those days. Whenever she came to see us, we found her restless and impatient. She was a part of the revolution and could not stand still for a moment. She had recently found a job at the planning office of the city council but she would leave her office in the middle of the day to go to political meetings. She was usually in the first row at demonstrations, where she boldly carried the leftist banners and shouted revolutionary slogans. Her use of these slogans in everyday discussions angered Amin. Nargess was always very polite and conservative in front of her brother, but Amin could detect certain political inclinations in her words, of which he did not approve.

Nargess soon realized that she could not come to an understanding with her brother on such matters. Therefore, she consciously tried not to engage in political discussions with him. This was totally against her nature. She was even frank with her father, who was amazed by his daughter's opinions about religion and revolution, as well as her never ending zeal. In the extended family, the only one who would approve of her positions was Saeed.

Nargess had recently begun to read forbidden books, translated pamphlets, and underground literature and to talk excitedly about a secretive world. Saeed was the one who had the key to this world and could introduce her to its secrets. She had asked Saeed to take her to meetings and provide her with publications. Saeed, though initially worried about her zealous excitement, soon found that she could be very wise and self-controlled as well. Thus, he was able to provide a cohesion and rationalization to the values Nargess had accepted through her sheer emotions, sensitivity, and self-sacrificing temperament. Nargess talked about Saeed as a teacher who had taught her a new way of life in a short span of time.

That Thursday afternoon, while I thought Nargess was talking about Saeed, I was actually coming to realize an irritating possibility that I had sensed for a long time, from the moment Margaret had left Iran. Nargess sat next to me on the sofa. I could see Amin's photo on the little table, staring at me, forcing me to say how happy I was for Nargess and Saeed.

"I am so happy, Nargess. Both for you and Saeed. He was very sad after what Maggie did to him," I said.

Nargess looked at me bewildered and then her pretty lips trembled in an unsuccessful attempt to control a sudden, loud laughter. She put her hand over her mouth and I heard her voice, muffled by her fingers. "Saeed? But I was not talking about Saeed. I am going with Ahmad!"

"Ahmad?"

"Yes…. Why are you so puzzled?"

I was surprised that she would travel with Ahmad. I knew that Ahmad was in love with her. Although he had never confessed it, everybody had observed his evident affections. But I had never seen Nargess pay any particular attention to him. I felt a sense of relief. I took a deep breath with a shiver of satisfaction. I tried not to look at Amin.

"Ahmad is a unique young man," I said.

Nargess toyed with her hair. "I came to know him during Amin's disappearance," she said. "There are certain special times when one finds a chance to get to know someone and become attracted to him. But why did you think I was in love with Saeed?"

"I don't know. Nowadays, you're always together. It seemed to me that Saeed was very fond of you." My voice was calm and controlled.

She laughed and leaned back, blocking my view of Amin's photo. "Of course he likes me. I like him too. But there is no love between us. Saeed is my friend and brother." Then she brought her face near mine and lowered her voice. "He is only in love with you!"

I was completely shocked. "Nonsense. Don't say such nonsense, Nargess. Saeed and I have been good friends for years. Even before I came to know Amin." My voice sounded furious.

Nargess leaned back again and her voice became serious. "He himself has told me that he has always been in love with you, but Amin took you from him."

I shifted and found Amin's eyes fixed on me. My words sounded angry. "That's a big lie. When I met Amin there was nothing between me and Saeed."

Nargess stood up in front of me. Her tight green dress added to her natural beauty. She looked at me angrily for a while. "Yes. I know that you had no relationship with Saeed. But Saeed had told Amin about his love for you. He told him that he was planning to propose to you but was waiting for your health to improve. But Amin used those very conditions to take you."

She was now looking straight in my eyes. "Luba, I know everything!"

I felt my heart sink like a broken wall, while a severe pain pushed its way into my chest. The first thing I could think of was Bardia's secret. But I could not possibly ask Nargess what she knew in that respect. I merely looked at her in total confusion.

"Amin is gone and will not return. You had better think of your own life, Luba."

I looked away from her and toward Amin. An unprecedented anger gushed inside my head. "Don't talk like that, Nargess. Even if Amin is gone for you, he is always with me. I love him and I want to keep this love for the rest of my life."

Nargess moved slowly toward me, bent down, and kissed my cheek. Then, without saying a word, she exited the room and left me with my ever-present fears, which now stood on much more logical grounds.

I heard her saying goodbye to Fatemeh Khanum. I wanted to run after her and ask if she knew that Bardia was not her brother's real son. But there was no energy left in me. I still believed in Saeed's faithfulness. But, as I reviewed what Nargess had told me I became convinced that he had told Bardia's secret to my sister-in-law. He could have told others, as well. For all I knew, everybody would soon know that Bardia was not Amin's son. If this became common knowledge, how would people behave toward Bardia? And what would Bardia himself do if he became aware of such a devastating fact? What about Esmat Khanum and Hajji?

I tried to recollect Nargess's recent behavior with Bardia. There was nothing unusual in it. Only once, when Bardia was talking to Sahand — Soraya's twelve year old son — about the fire and the horrible snakes which engulf the sinful people in hell, and Nargess and I could hear his voice coming from the garden, she told me, "I think you should take Bardia to your place as soon as possible. What he says worries me a lot."

Was she actually preparing grounds for sending Bardia out of a house belonging to people who had no blood relation to him? And, today, when she told me that I should think about my own life, did she mean that Hajji and his wife knew the truth and would not look at me with the same eyes anymore? Considering the love Nargess had for her brother, how could she talk about him like that? How could she talk about another man's love for her brother's wife?

It took me two torturous hours to realize that the wisest solution was to ask Saeed about the truth. I asked Fatemeh Khanum to go home earlier than usual and telephoned Saeed at his office. I asked him to come to see me that evening.

.9.

It was late in the evening when Saeed arrived with two bottles of homemade vodka. The bottles were wrapped in newspaper. He unwrapped them and placed them on the table. "Albert brought a few of these today. These are your share."

He didn't know that I had not had to wait so long for Albert's vodkas. From my colleagues at work, I had managed to get a few bottles of vodka, made in Eastern Europe and sold in the black markets of Tehran. Without looking at Saeed, I went to the kitchen and brought back some hors d'oeuvres with two glasses, set them on the table and sat opposite Amin's photo. "Nargess was here today. She was going to Golsara."

"She said she'd take you, too," he laughed. "It seems that she wasn't successful."

I looked at him. His large, mystery-ridden eyes — the best features of his face — were gently focused on me.

"I wasn't in the mood for such a trip. I'm not in the mood for anything."

He opened one of the bottles and poured for both of us.

"I'm glad that you were in the mood to see me today."

He looked up, straight into my eyes. I avoided his gaze and took the glass.

"Have you told Nargess about Bardia?"

His hands, moving the glass toward his mouth, stopped in mid-air. His eyes bore an inquisitive and bewildered look.

"What about him?"

I unintentionally looked down.

"Does Nargess know that he is not Amin's son?"

Saeed was clearly shocked. He put his glass back on the table.

"Of course not. Why do you ask?"

I felt relieved and leaned back.

"Oh my God, I have been going mad since this afternoon."

Puzzled, Saeed was still looking at me and waiting for some kind of explanation.

"Nargess was talking about how I had met Amin. She had heard the story from you. So I was afraid you might have told her about Bardia, as well."

He sipped his drink and lit a cigarette. Looking at the gray evening sky through the widow, he murmured softly.

"I'm sorry that you thought that."

I wanted to take him in my arms and cover his face with kisses.

"I'm so ashamed, Saeed. These days I've been suspicious about everything."

He laughed.

"Don't you ever become suspicious about me. Forget it, Luba. Tell me about yourself."

But I didn't want to change the subject. A mysterious desire forced me to say something I hadn't intended to say. I cast a hasty glance at the photo of Amin.

"You told Nargess that you were in love with me when I met Amin."

A rush of blood flushed his high forehead. He looked away and gazed at Amin's photo. There was a momentary pause between us.

"I don't understand why she would have told you this," he said.

I was quick to answer back.

"I don't understand why you would have told her. And I don't know if it has a grain of truth to it. Even if it is true, why would you tell her something that could change her opinion about her brother? I don't approve of what you've done."

He raised his head and looked at me.

"I didn't want to change her opinion about Amin. I mentioned my love for you during a friendly chat. That's all."

My heart beat turbulently. I did not know if it was because of excitement or anger. But, when I opened my mouth, I noticed that my voice was full of fury.

"Nargess has accepted that Amin told me about his own love despite the fact that he knew you loved me. But you know that he was too honorable to do such a thing."

Saeed looked down at the carpet. He was squeezing his glass so hard that I thought it would break. But when he began to talk, his voice was calm.

"It is not important anymore whether or not you accept it. Perhaps if Amin had not died, I never would have told you. I wouldn't have told Nargess, either. But I did tell Amin about my love for you the very night I took you to the hospital. I told him that I intended to tell you once your child was born. But he stalled me after Bardia was born."

He gazed straight into my eyes.

"You see? I did tell him, Luba. What do you call what he did?"

I anxiously attempted an answer.

"Perhaps he didn't believe you were serious. Perhaps.... And what about me? Was I a baby doll? Wasn't it my right to choose my own man?"

Saeed put his glass down on the table and lit another cigarette.

"If I had indeed seen you as a doll, I would have confronted Amin in another way. I respected your choice. But I never could forget that Amin was not a straightforward man."

His voice was trembling. I answered again with an anger not familiar even to myself.

"But you never liked Amin, did you? Even before I met him."

Saeed put his cigarette box and his lighter in his pocket. I knew that he intended to leave. I knew that whenever he became annoyed or angry, he would leave. But he didn't. He stood there in front of me, looking straight into my eyes. His face was red and his eyes were fixed in an intense stare. He was almost shouting.

"Yes, you're right. I never liked him. I actually hated him. I resented him so much."

He continued while pointing to Amin's photo.

"I wish I could...."

I was shocked.

"But Amin had not done anything wrong to you."

The words came out of my mouth involuntarily. Saeed, like an angry animal caught in a cage, began to move around the room without paying any attention to what I was saying.

"When I saw his dead body, I did not have any pity for him. I cried, but not for him."

Saeed's behavior puzzled me. I thought that I had been unreasonably rude to him. I wished I could calm him. I wished I could ask him to sit down. But I was unable to do so. The same mysterious feeling prevented me to say what I wanted to say.

"I never thought that you could be so irrational," I said.

He stood still, then slowly came toward me. He was not the Saeed I knew. He had the face of a child who was not yet going to surrender, even after a long cry.

"But Amin was so rational; he never became angry. He always smiled and was always happy to chat. You were right to choose him. You were right to love him. Everybody loved him. You were right; everybody else was right. It was only me who hated him. Only me."

He left the room without waiting for my reaction. A moment later I heard the front door close with a loud bang.

His behavior totally confused me. I could not understand why I was not angered by what he had said or why I was not glad that he left. Instead, I noticed that there was a distinctly pleasant feeling inside of me. I poured a drink and sat on the rocking chair in front of the window, my back to Amin's photo. I tried to attribute the feeling to the fact that Bardia's secret had not been disclosed after all.

• • • • •

I woke up late on Friday morning. Soraya's call awakened me. She wanted to know if I was all right and if I had any special plans for the day. I told her that I was free; I had only to go to Hajji's place to pick up the children late in the evening. Soraya wasn't busy, either. Abdol had taken Sahand to see his grandfather. She suggested we meet for a few hours, so I invited her for lunch. Once out of bed, I noticed that the skin under my eyes was bluish and puffy. I tried to cover it with make-up, perhaps hide from Soraya's keen eyes.

I had known Soraya for thirteen years — since she had married Abdol and moved from Scotland to London. During my first year of marriage, I had not seen Abdol, but Amin talked about him often. I knew Amin considered him a brother and that Hajji Jalali loved Abdol and his sister, Homeira, as his own children. Abdol's father, Colonel Javad Nuri, was one of Hajji's childhood friends and, as Hajji said, they had considered each other as brothers from that early age on. After high school, Javad Nuri chose to serve in the military and Hajji became a businessman in the bazaar. This occupational separation had not affected their relationship; in fact, they joked about each other's occupation. Hajji jokingly called his friend "General Nuri" and Javad addressed the young businessman as "Hajji Agha."

In the beginning of the 1950s, however, when nationalist fervor overcame the political scene in Iran under the leadership of Mossadegh, the colonel joined the underground section of the Tudeh Communist Party inside the military and Hajji became involved in the political activities of the National Front. Thus, they had ended up in opposite ends of the Iranian political spectrum. They seldom saw each other and whenever they met, their political differences turned their meetings into bitter confrontations. Then came the coup d'etat of 1953 and the fall of Mossadegh, as well as the return of the Shah to Iran to begin his ride to absolute dictatorship. Colonel Nuri was arrested and imprisoned. It was during this period that Hajji assumed the responsibility of raising the colonel's two children.

The colonel was twice sentenced to death by firing squad and was saved miraculously. Then he was exiled to the deserted Kish Island in the Persian Gulf and spent twelve years in miserable conditions. While there, he lost both legs to severe gangrene. His wife, Afagh, applied for a divorce three years after the colonel's arrest. She declared that she did not want to be the wife of someone who was convicted as a "traitor to his country." Soon after the divorce, she remarried and left Iran with her new husband. Abdol and Homeira were given to the colonel's mother and Hajji continued his financial and parental support. This support continued even when the colonel was released and became housebound in Tehran. During his absence, Hajji had sent Abdol to study in England and had found Homeira a suitable husband. Hajji's financial aid to Abdol had continued until two years before I met Abdol, when he had finished his studies in computer science.

When Abdol and Soraya came to live in London, we soon became good friends. We even went to Iran together. I was fond of Soraya from our very first meeting. She was a pleasant and gentle woman, with a small body and miniature features. She was not an outstanding beauty, but she attracted others' attention with her delicate and wise behavior. She was very successful at her job, as well. Both in England and Iran, her patients almost immediately trusted her; this made it easier for her to attend to their difficulties. Apart from Saeed and Amin, she was the only one whom I had told what I had gone through in my own country, although I never revealed Bardia's secret to her. She was quite familiar with my psychology, then, and could recognize my moods without any evident clues.

It was not surprising that a few minutes after Soraya arrived at my apartment, as I was putting the food on the table, she said, "You're in a mess, Luba. Don't you think it's time for you to do something about it?"

After a few moments I realized that Saeed had told her about my physical and mental conditions, without mentioning what had happened between us the night before. He must have told her about my sinking eyes and trembling hands. He had probably remarked that Amin's absence had devastated me.

I suddenly realized that my day had become a continuation of the previous night. I didn't know if I should thank Saeed or become angrier because of this intrusion.

Saeed had also told Soraya something else that he had thought might be useful to Soraya if she was going to help me. Now Soraya, who had been alerted to my condition, was here in my home to see if she could be of any help at all. I shrugged off her question.

"What else can I do?"

"You should live. As you used to do before."

" I am alive. Can't you see?

"No. Don't fool yourself. You cannot call this a proper way of living. You've turned into a ghost who has nobody but Amin's ghost to live with. It is as if you want to kill yourself to join him. To join someone whom you didn't love when he was alive."

She uttered the last words in the manner of an archer shooting an arrow right into the heart of the target. I jumped up as if stricken by lightning.

"I've always loved Amin. Always."

She was quite indifferent to my reaction.

"You like to think that you've always loved him. You feel more convenient this way. But, to do so, you have to resort to alcohol and tranquilizers. You have to force yourself to sit and think about him throughout the night."

My laughter was a nervous outbreak. I felt that, at least in her eyes, my face had turned into the face of a lunatic.

"These are just your psychoanalytical contemplations, my dear Freud!"

But there was no sign of her backing down.

"No. These are not my contemplations. Look at your face, at your sinking eyes with those bluish areas around them. Look at your fingers, which tremble with the tiniest excitement. They tell me about your condition. Nargess tells me that you are becoming an aggressive person. Ahmad says that whenever he comes to see you, he finds you stretched on the floor with Amin's photos and family albums scattered around you. Look at this place. This is not a home. This is a museum of Amin's memories. Just tell me if all of these pictures in every corner of this place could be the work of a normal mind."

I put my head between my hands. I wished I could cry loudly. But it had been a long time since my eyes had dropped a tear. I was totally helpless.

"I don't know. I don't know what to know. I cannot escape from Amin's memory for a moment."

"Of course you can. You could if you wanted to. I have always considered you a wise and strong woman. You have to accept the fact that Amin is dead. He is now like any other material body. He is not better than any one of them."

I raised my head.

"But the difference is that this one was the only one I had. He was my everything. I believe that he was the only one who cared about me. He gave me back a life after I had lost sixteen years. And now his death makes me feel that I have no past at all. Nothing. I look back and see a man with no faults whom I valued less than he deserved when he was alive."

Soraya fell silent. I couldn't read her face, but I could tell that she was on the verge of telling me something that she found too difficult to say. She ate her last morsel of food and stood up to walk around the room. After a while she turned around and looked at me.

"It is your mind that has created such a faultless person out of Amin. These are fabrications brought about by his death. Otherwise, you would undoubtedly know that he was not such a perfect man. He had so many shortcomings from which you used to suffer."

Soraya, seeing that I was about to protest, motioned me to remain silent and continued.

"Let's consider examples. What would you say if you knew that he had one or a few mistresses? Would you still love him and believe in his impeccability? Or, let's suppose that on the very day he disappeared, he had operated on his own mistress to abort his own child. Would you still think that he was a perfect husband?"

After the last word, she sat down right in front of me and cast her penetrating eyes on my confused expression. It was as if she was evaluating the impact of what she had told me. I did not like her story at all and turned my face away.

"How could one reject a person because of odd assumptions?"

Soraya smiled bitterly, and while keeping her eyes on me, answered back.

"These are not assumptions. They constitute the truth — the truth which Saeed knew but didn't have the courage to say."

It seemed to me that Soraya and Saeed had conspired to help me by creating this absurd scenario. I laughed in anger and raised my voice.

"Soraya, you don't need to disgrace Amin in order to help me. I thought people like you would know better ways to help people."

Soraya put her hand on my knee. The tears in her eyes bewildered me.

"I'm not a fool, Luba…. I don't wish to disgrace Amin. I don't consider what I'm doing as disgracing someone. What I told you is true; you had to know it sooner or later."

The only thing that popped up in my mind was that at last I was going to find that woman. I heard my voice coming out of a hollow space, so faint that I could hardly hear it myself.

"Tell me who this woman is."

Soraya was relieved. My reaction clearly satisfied her. She answered me while leaning back.

"I don't know."

I was struggling in an endless void. There was no love or hate in me. I bent toward her and heard my pleading voice.

"Tell me…. I beg you, tell me all of the details."

"I don't know, Luba. I swear that I don't know anything more. Out of the whole story, this is what Saeed chose to tell me. He says that this woman is now outside of Iran. It seems that no one among us knew her."

"Is she related to Amin's death?"

"No. Saeed says that the woman herself told him everything."

I felt like I was hearing everything in a nightmare. There was a shiver in my back which crawled up to my neck and retreated again. I was not thinking about that unknown woman any more. She was now a real person, a woman who was Amin's mistress, whom he had impregnated. From the bottom of my heart, I wished to talk to this woman or, at least, hear more about her. I murmured in a faint voice.

"I have to know everything about this woman."

"What difference would it make?"

"A lot. I need to know more about her."

Soraya's eyes, now dry, were fixed on me.

"If you think it would help, do so. Talk to Saeed."

.10.

On Sunday at noon, the American Embassy was taken over by a group of young men who called themselves "Student Followers of the Imam." I heard the news while dining with my colleagues at the museum. No one had heard anything about this group before. It seemed that the name was created after the takeover. For the next day, everybody talked about this incident. There was no doubt that such an incident could have grave political consequences for Iran. Everyone believed that Americans would not keep silent. We expected a severe reaction, and perhaps some sort of military intervention. Some believed that the transitional government was not involved but that extremist groups inside the regime, led by a Mullah, who was known to have connections with the Soviet Union, were responsible for what had happened; if so, the government would soon interfere and release the hostages. There were others, who saw everything as a play staged by the U.S., in order to fortify the religious government's power.

I felt that this was happening on another planet, far from me. I was not curious about what was happening. I had left Soraya like a zombie, picked up the children, and, for two whole days, I had remained at home, unaware of the grave storm whirling in the streets of Tehran. That woman had stolen my soul; to restore my life, I had to find her.

The political storm which had attacked Iran prevented me from seeing Saeed for a while. I didn't call him Saturday because I was ashamed of the way I had behaved. On Sunday I was unable to find him. Nargess, who had returned from Golsara Saturday evening, was also not accessible. Ahmad told me that they were engaged in the preparation of a pamphlet about the unexpected takeover of the American Embassy.

Upon my arrival at home, Bardia who usually spent his time in his room, welcomed me by happily telling me about the takeover of the embassy. He added that his headmaster was going to take the children to the front of the embassy, where they would participate in demonstrations. Bardia was to carry the school flag.

Initially amazed by his excitement over the takeover, I suddenly became furious about the demonstration. I uncontrollably began to shout at him.

"You are not going to this demonstration. You do not have my permission."

Bardia, who was not expecting this reaction, was shocked. Without a word, he ran into his room and slammed the door. This was the first time I had reacted this way to anyone. The children had not seen me shout before. My hands were shaking and I could hear my own deep, irregular breaths. Bahram had squeezed himself into a corner and was on the verge of crying, with his frightened eyes fixed on me. I felt sorry for him. I sat down on the floor and asked Fatemeh Khanum, who was staring at me in a puzzled manner, to bring me my tranquilizer tablets. It took me a while to regain control. Bahram was still frightened and crouched in the corner. I went toward him and took him in my arms.

That night Bardia did not come out of his room for dinner. Fatemeh Khanum brought food to his room, but he left it untouched.

I went to bed feeling guilty and in pain. I could not sleep at all. It was early in the morning when the effects of my third tranquilizer began to hit me and I surrendered myself to a deep sleep that continued until noon.

It was an autumn afternoon. The sun was hazy. I felt confused and bewildered. I poured myself a cup of coffee and called the museum. The man at the switchboard told me that all governmental offices were nearly empty and half were closed. His voice was full of a rare excitement. "Everybody has gone for the demonstration," he said.

I asked Fatemeh Khanum about the children. Clearly worried, she told me that when she had arrived early in the morning she had seen Bardia leaving the apartment. He had told her that he was going to participate in the demonstration. She had taken Bahram to school and had no other news.

Bardia's decision startled me. Although I was amazed by his courage to disobey me, the main cause of my worries was the unpredictability of the demonstration. I thought I should try to find him, but I couldn't find enough energy to do so. I sent Fatemeh Khanum to fetch Bahram and, feeling totally helpless, telephoned Hajji, whom I knew would be home for lunch. I told him what had happened. He was clearly furious and his voice was trembling.

"I don't know why these bunch of fools are doing this. Or why they involve the children."

He paused for a while and then, as if just realizing that I was waiting for his decision at the other end of the line, continued.

"Don't worry, Luba. This is not going to be a dangerous demonstration. I'll send Majid immediately to find him."

Early in the evening, Esmat Khanum telephoned to tell me that Bardia was with her. She wanted my permission to keep him there for the night. I could not do anything but accept. Fortunately, Ahmad had been with me since the early afternoon. His college was also closed, and his students had gone to the demonstration. He spoke in a puzzled but compassionate tone.

"I don't know what has happened to these kids. They used to hate the idea of a religious state, but now they applaud the Imam and approve and cheer politically illogical actions."

Although Ahmad's political views were similar to those of Saeed and Nargess, he rejected their repeated invitations for him to join their organization.

"Art is not compatible with political organizations," he would say. "I don't like to paint according to the guidelines given to me by this or that group." Nargess attributed Ahmad's attitude to his familial background. She often pointed to the fact that Ahmad was born in a Bahá'í family. Bahá'ís were always considered renegades by the official Iranian religion and were persecuted by the new regime. Ahmad, who denied this implication with good humor, had once answered Nargess in a very serious tone. "I have taken from my family background as much as you've taken from yours."

Ahmad was seventeen years old when he escaped from his wealthy family, who resided in Shiraz in the south of Iran. He could not tolerate his family's strict adherence to religious belief and ceremony. He came to Tehran and worked and studied simultaneously for fourteen years. Nevertheless, his family had not forsaken him. After the victory of the revolution and the massacre of the Bahá'ís, his whole family decided to leave Iran. They had tried their best to convince Ahmad to go with them, but he preferred to stay in Iran. During recent years, especially when the uprisings began, he gained a respectable reputation as a painter, and his exhibitions were always welcomed by art critics and young enthusiasts. This had not affected his shy, modest, and unpretentious personality. He taught at the Faculty of Fine Arts for a few hours per week and spent most of his time painting at home. He was usually reluctant to meet others and had a very limited circle of friends. Sometimes I felt that he had even fewer friends than me, a stranger in this country.

That evening, I remembered to congratulate Ahmad on his new relationship with Nargess. His grayish eyes seemed brighter than ever. He combed his sleek black hair aside with his fingers and spoke shyly.

"I still cannot believe it. I was sure, even up to last week, that Nargess paid no attention to me. I was so sure of this that I had never even contemplated telling her about my feelings."

With a childish giddiness, he told me that Nargess had arrived at his apartment without prior notice. "I'm getting bored with your silent gaze," she had said. "It's high time you tell me what's on your mind." In lieu of words, Ahmad had shown her his last painting, which he had created exclusively for her. Nargess had laughed and said, "Your paintings are as mute as your tongue!"

I saw that painting when it was finished. Nargess eventually took it to her house. It depicted a woman in a red gown, standing on a hill covered by green grass. One of her hands pointed to a river roaring down the hill. A faint fog had blended the aspects of the picture together. Only the river and the woman's eyes, similar to those of Nargess, shone in the mist. If you looked at the painting from a distance you would only see those two eyes and the river.

•　•　•　•　•

October, the peak of Tehran's autumn, was pulsating in a ceaseless rhythm. A partially cloudy sky shifted the broken yellow rays of sun, colorful trees shed their leaves to carpet the alleys and streets, a zephyr similar to the spring breezes of the Atlantic coast swept the masses of leaves, changing every corner of the city into the work of a lunatic painter. The sleepy streets were awakened by flags, banners and a slogan that repeated, "Death to America." The streets were constantly crowded and the clamor of newspaper boys, always reporting news of President Carter's endeavors to release the hostages, seemed like an unending stream. The lines of daily demonstrations crossed the veins of Tehran and, once reaching the center of town, suddenly coagulated into a whirling, pulsating pool. The students who occupied the American Embassy, were armed to the teeth. They were always present on the roof and walls of the building. The eyes of teenagers and elderly men glowed with a similar light. Fueled by the regime's systematic propaganda, excitement and passion permeated the streets. Everybody was waiting for something to happen, and everyone had constructed their own versions.

"They'll surrender the Shah and his wealth to Iran."

"The hostages won't be released unless Israel returns the occupied lands to the Palestinians."

"Americans are preparing themselves to invade Iran."

"Soviets won't remain silent. Soon they'll occupy the northern part of Iran and Americans will settle in the south."

The young boys talked about the takeover as if they occupied the actual United States and had taken all Americans hostage.

Bardia was one of these boys. He suddenly emerged from his cocoon of solitude in the shape of an energetic, thundering young man. The fact that he had disobeyed me to go to the demonstration yet had not been punished led him to show up in front of the embassy every afternoon and evening. Every day, upon returning home, he had a new gift for Bahram in the form of a new slogan.

The only one who openly opposed all of this was Hajji Jalali. Whenever we were at his house, he spoke as if to all of us, but his words were aimed at Bardia.

"These protests are a mistake. They only can discredit us in the world. How on earth can you enter people's houses and then arrest them? These are acts of lawlessness. They have committed nothing less than armed robbery."

Bardia, who understood Hajji's implications, always had his answers ready.

"This is not a house or an embassy. This is the nest of spies."

Hajji tried to be gentle and kind.

"Don't say such things, my son. The world has its own laws. Even to enter the house of a thief, you must have the permission of the public prosecutor. Couldn't they close the embassy and ask the Americans to leave this country?"

Bardia had the attitude of a creditor speaking to someone who was trying to deny him his debts.

"So that they could take their important and valuable documents with them?"

Hajji spoke sternly.

"You are so naive, my boy. Why would they keep their important documents in the embassy? Even if such documents were there, the Americans could have taken them out of the country on the eve of the revolution. Your thoughts are childish."

Bardia tried to stop the discussion by remaining silent for the rest of the visit. But, the next day he went to the demonstration to bring new slogans home.

I was completely oblivious to whatever was happening around me. I heard the words but I was unable to understand them. At night, when the children were asleep, I sat down in the kitchen and drank smuggled vodka. Later, I took sleeping pills and stretched out on the bed, unaware of my surroundings. The next day, dizzy and staggering, I went back to the Iranian Archeological Museum.

There was no news from Saeed. He had gone to Kurdistan the week of the takeover. In my daydreams, I tried to picture Amin's mistress, but I could never formulate even the vaguest features.

I didn't want to see anybody. Whenever someone asked to come over, I came up with an excuse to refuse. Only on Friday evenings would I go to Hajji's house to pick up the children. I would stay there for a few hours. My hellish solitude at home was broken only by occasional visits by Nargess and Ahmad. They would arrive without any notice, sit in my home for a few hours, and then leave.

Later on, Nargess told me that she was so worried about me during those days and had contacted Soraya to ask for help. But Soraya, not knowing that Nargess also knew of the existence of the unknown woman, could not do much. I, too, was not in the mood to see Soraya before I saw Saeed. She could not do anything for me. Once she had told Nargess, "It would have been easier for Luba to leave Amin if he was still alive. But now she believes she could not leave a dead man." Nargess was not able to understand what she was talking about.

Soraya didn't exactly understand me, either. I wished Amin was alive, even for one day. But not so I could leave him; I wanted to stand in front of him and tell him in person that I had never loved him, that I had never even enjoyed sleeping with him.

But why? Why had I never told him so before? Why had I not told him what I used to feel during those several nights when he would lie on top of me for cold, brief intercourse, and then fall asleep a few moments later, stretched on his back like a victorious warlord? Why hadn't I told him that there had not been a night when I hadn't disentangled myself from his arms, unsatisfied and disappointed? There had not been a single night when, as his first deep breaths turned into a childish snore, I did not shed muffled tears into my pillow. Why hadn't I told him that I still longed for a bit of that pleasure that I had experienced in my two other relationships when I was a young girl?

I knew that Amin was not going to return. Therefore, my thoughts focused on the unknown woman more than ever. I wanted to say these things to that woman, as if she were his representative in the world of the living. I only wished to find her; the key to finding her, I thought, would be Saeed.

• • • • •

Tasu'a (the ninth day of the month of *Moharram* in the Shi'ite calendar) fell on a rainy Wednesday. According to Shi'ite tradition, on such a night 1,400 years ago, Imam Hossein, the third leader of the Shi'ites, gathered with his family in the Karbala Desert (inside present-day Iraq). They were preparing for a bloody war at the break of dawn on the tenth day (*Ashura*) during which the Imam and all of his male relatives except for his son were to be massacred. The Shi'ites were still very determined to keep this myth of sacred martyrdom alive in

Iran. From the afternoon onward, the sad wailing of the many marchers could be heard from the street. During the seemingly ceaseless procession, men in black shirts divided into small groups with separate flags and banners.

The schools were closed for three days for the occasion, so Bardia and Bahram stayed at Hajji's place. Hajji made a yearly contribution to the religious ceremony. He opened the door of his house to the public and ordered his cooks to prepare food for the mourners of the martyred Imam. Throngs of men in black shirts would come inside, beating their chests and reciting elegies. Once the food was ready, they would stand in the garden and eat their dinner in silence. After they consumed the food, they left the house the same way they had entered it. Every year, Amin, the children, and I would go to Hajji's for the occasion. I always went out of interest and Amin went out of respect for his parents. With my children at my side, I would stand in the window and watch the ceremony.

This year I had not gone, even for a few hours. But the children were enthusiastic to go. Bardia dressed completely in black, just like the men in the processions, and I could imagine him standing amid them, beating his young chest with the rhythm of the eulogy, accompanied by the cymbal.

It was nearly eight o'clock when I heard knocks at the door. I thought it might be Nargess or Ahmad checking up on me. But when I opened the door, I found Saeed standing there, with his face and hair full of raindrops.

I welcomed him with a rare smile. "*Cheh ajab!*"

I used a Persian phrase that roughly meant "What a surprise." Because it was mostly a colloquial expression, Saeed, as he had always done in the past, burst into laughter. Although I could speak Persian very well, the way I pronounced the words made others laugh. When I first arrived in Iran, I tried my best not to use such odd expressions. But, later on, I came to realize that people laughed at me out of joy and not condescension. From then on, I usually used these expressions on purpose to make people laugh. That night, of course, I was not in the mood for such amusement. I spoke the phrase without thinking.

Saeed hung his raincoat on a hanger. As he entered the living room, he was taken aback by the chaotic scene: a few partly eaten morsels of cheese and vegetables, a half-empty bottle of vodka, and a half-filled glass.

"Have you finished or are you going to start?"

I didn't want him to know that the food had been sitting there untouched since the night before. I had even begun to drink my vodka without eating any food.

"I was going to start."

When he looked at me, I immediately realized that he knew I was lying.

"So I arrived at the right time," he said.

He went to the kitchen and found himself a plate and a glass. Then he sat opposite me.

"Apparently, I came on the right night, as well. You cannot find such vodka anywhere in the city, even at Albert's place."

It was as if we had not had such an ugly confrontation at our last meeting. He seemed calm and comfortable. I was silent. He put a piece of cutlet on my plate.

"I missed you a lot. It's been such a long time since I last saw you. Nargess said you'd been looking for me."

He knew exactly why I was looking for him.

"When Amin was alive, we saw more of you."

There was anger in my voice, but I was not sure why. Saeed's eyes were shining, but they were faintly shadowed by exhaustion. He didn't pay any attention to what I had implied.

"Troubles are on the rise. Some of our comrades were arrested and if they send them to Tehran, they could certainly end up in front of the firing squads."

"So what did you do?"

"We could release them…. with difficulty and by bribing people in the local committees."

"What was their charge?"

Saeed smiled bitterly.

"They were distributing our publications. These days, it is a grave risk to oppose this business of taking people hostage. You know that they don't have any principles or logical reasons for their actions. We say that they have orchestrated this act to suppress the opposition. They say we are American spies."

He laughed and sipped the rest of his drink. He continued talking about political issues for awhile. Although I had been looking forward to talking to him, I preferred to remain silent and listen to what he was saying. Actually, I did not know when or how to begin. But, at last, I broke my silence.

"It is very good that you are so hopeful and active."

He smiled and poured himself another drink.

"Why not? Is there any other purpose for our lives?"

"Good for you. It's nice that you can think like that."

Saeed suddenly stopped playing with his food and moved to the edge of the sofa. He seemed to be about to say something important.

"You could think like that, too. During the first few months we were friends, I told myself that if we had a handful of women like you in our country, the social situation would be totally different. Despite all those hardships you had suffered, you were full of hope and passion. You had a thousand plans for your future. You intended to wait for your child to be born so that you could become free to inform the whole world about the ordeals of your countrymen. Do you remember all that? Do you remember what exciting plans you had in mind? I learned a lot from you. I was so happy to know a person like you."

I did not want him to talk about the past. It was as if he was talking about a dead woman. Her name and her memories were tormenting me. I had to interrupt him.

"The past belongs to the past."

He looked straight into my eyes.

"Look, Luba. One day we promised each other we would remain good friends and rush to each other's aid wherever we might be in the world...."

We were standing on the bridge, looking at the river Thames, which reflected a scattered array of London lights. The night emphasized the enchanting beauty of the river; its dirty water was not detectable in the darkness. A few moments ago, we had just come out of a theater. I had been pregnant with Bardia for eight months. I wrapped my overcoat tightly around my body so my unborn child wouldn't feel cold. He had raised a tumult inside of me, playfully pounding his arms and feet in my womb and distracting my attention from the beauty of the scene. I felt that his brittle fingers reached toward my breasts and played around my heart. His feet, dragging on the inside of my womb, charged some kind of sexual pleasure into my blood. My hands, inside my pocket, caressed my belly in search of his head. I could not find it at first. But, as soon as I began to get worried, the baby gently pounded on my belly. Saeed was standing next to me. I wished I could take his hands and place them on my belly. "See? Here. Here, where it moves. It is his hand. His head is here and his foot is there."

His name was not yet Bardia. Amin would later give him that name. I intended to call him Chorka. For the duration of the play, he was calm. But there, on the bridge, the cold weather had made him restless. I wrapped the overcoat more tightly around myself. "Don't be cold, my little one. Don't be cold."

I restlessly stood up, left the room, and opened the door to Bardia's room. The light in the hall hardly illuminated anything inside the room. Only his empty bed was detectable in the faint light. Something was pounding in my empty womb. I closed the door, went to my room, took a sweater, and returned to the living room. Saeed looked at me, confused.

"Sorry. I suddenly felt cold," I said.

With the sweater on my shoulders, I sat down in front of him. Saeed smiled.

"Are you all right, Luba?"

I had asked him if we could go somewhere to sit. Saeed pointed to a cafe a short walk away. And we had gone there. While at the table, Saeed asked if I had enjoyed Macbeth.

"Of course I enjoyed it. I have seen it before, in Prague, in a closed theater. It was done very modestly there."

Saeed was puzzled. "What is a closed theater?"

"A woman named Huisova called her house a closed theater. When the regime prohibited her from appearing on stage, she took her theater into her home. It was a tiny place, but thirty to forty people could squeeze themselves inside the room to watch her plays."

Saeed was excited. "Didn't police know about this?"

"Of course they knew. They were always around her house, but they had no plausible reason to stop her. One night they did indeed attack the place and arrested her with the other actors. They were performing the same play we watched tonight. They'd found a valid reason in one sentence of the play: 'Night is long and no day would find the day.'"

"Were you there on that night?"

"No. I was there the night before with my father. Huisova was a close friend of his."

Saeed had said, "You have to write this all on paper. It is important that you write down what has happened to you and to your country."

"I'm not a writer," I had answered. "But I often feel that while I'm enjoying the benefits of freedom, there are thousands of Lubas still in that country who are suffering like I suffered. I know I should do something, but I don't know what. I suppose that writing could be a solution, one of the solutions...."

Saeed was overwhelmed. He had placed his hands on mine and said, "How nice that you think like that." Bardia suddenly pounded his legs on my loins. I moaned. Saeed stood up, came towards me and grabbed my arm.

"Are you all right, Luba?"

"Yes. I'm all right."

"Shall we go to a doctor?"

"No."

"Don't be shy, Luba. If you need...." and Bardia suddenly became calm, dancing gently in his world. He moved his hands along my ribs, playing an invisible harp. I laughed.

"I'm not shy. I'm so comfortable with you. I know that you're a real friend and I can rely on you." I immediately detested the thought of relying on someone else. A certain kind of pride thus shaped my next sentence. "But remember, I'm your friend, too. You can rely on me, as well." Saeed smiled and returned to his place.

Then, in almost a childish tone, he said, "Let's promise each other to keep our friendship forever. Nothing should come between us, even if we end up living miles apart." I didn't like his hint about such separation. Perhaps, until that moment, I had considered all he did for me as signs of love; in my mind, love was incompatible with distance.

I nervously stood up and said, "Agreed. I promise." Bardia restarted pounding his head on my belly. I moaned and asked Saeed to take me to a doctor.

I wanted to say, "It seems the devil decided to contaminate everything that night." This was a Czech expression my father used whenever he wanted to refer to the coup d'etat of February 1948, which brought Stalinists to power and handed my country over to dictators. But I only said, "I wished you hadn't taken me to that hospital."

Saeed looked down and, ignoring my comment, said, "Why have you done this to yourself? Only because your husband wasn't faithful to you?"

I hastily said, "No," and refilled my glass.

He put his hand on my knee. The warmth of his hand on my skirt rushed under my skin. "Be calm, Luba…. Talk to me…. Listen to me."

He took his hand away. I felt cold and squeezed myself into the sweater. He continued, "Do you remember, Luba? One day Milan said he didn't want to live with you any more, and he went away. A few days later, when you went together to get a divorce, you did not even ask him why he was doing so. Weren't you in love with him? Couldn't he have gone away because of another woman?"

After Milan's departure, throughout the days I was hidden in a stable near the border, and during the first months of my stay in England, I had asked myself why he had left. Just a few nights before, he asked for a divorce, he had held me in his arms with his usual warmth and passion; he had kissed me and had made love to me. Why had he suddenly turned into a piece of ice, an impenetrable piece of stone, to tell me only, "I'm sorry Luba, we have to be apart." Why had he so hurriedly placed the divorce documents in front of me with his signature already on it? Since that day, I had repeatedly asked myself why I had not asked him his reasons the divorce. But what difference would it have made? Whatever the reason, I knew that I had to be separated from someone I loved so dearly.

Saeed was watching me attentively.

"But he went away. He did not stay to cheat on me. He didn't remain with me while seeing a mistress."

Saeed leaned back and put his head against the cushion. He was so lovable in that gesture, as he looked at me with half-closed eyes.

"But you were able to throw him out of your life and mind. Why don't you want to do the same thing with Amin? Until a month ago, you were mourning because you had lost a dear husband and a faithful lover. Okay. But what about now? Are you mourning because he wasn't faithful to you or ever really in love with you?"

There was no hint of teasing in his words, but they still annoyed me.

"Don't hurt me so much, Saeed. Amin is not in my life anymore. I have given him up. But he hasn't left me. His shadow is cast over my life. By dying, he has denied me the chance to thrust my anger and hatred at his face. He won't let me see whatever has been kept hidden from me for so long…. By dying, he has denied me the chance to discover his lies."

"But you're wrong. The dead are less able to hide their lies than the living."

"You could be right. But not in your country, where they sanctify the dead and no one dares utter a derogatory word about them. Amin is even above all of that. He is a martyr. To you, a martyr is an innocent person, even if he is the dirtiest and worst one of all."

"You're right. You're absolutely right." Saeed was gentle and compromising. "But what else don't you know that you could know if Amin was alive?"

"I want to know who that other woman is. I want to know his mistress. I need to know her…. I need it. Believe me Saeed. There is nothing more horrible than knowing I've been cheated and I'm unable to tell the cheater that I know. Yes, it's too late, but at least I know what you've done. And, therefore, I'm not a fool."

"But Amin is not here. Nothing would change, even if you do find that woman."

"Yes. It will change a lot of things. I can tell Amin that I now know everything. Although he is dead and a martyr, I've discovered who his mistress was. He was not able to hide her from me."

A smiling Saeed was looking at me as if watching a little child. I leaned back and, using the remainder of the adrenaline pumped into my blood by the alcohol, continued to talk.

"Perhaps I'm deceiving myself. Perhaps I want to compare myself to that woman. I don't know. Believe me, I don't know."

Saeed remained silent for a while. Then he lit a cigarette. There was no smile on his lips anymore. He did not even look at me, so I could watch him unobserved. The smoke, in circles, came out of his large lips — half hidden under his thick mustache — blew around his nose, still crooked from an old break, and scattered in front of his face. As I watched him, he suddenly surprised me with his final decision.

"I'll tell you who that woman is tonight!"

I was shocked but I did not have enough energy to move. Saeed stared straight into my eyes.

"But you have to give me your word before I say anything."

My answer was quick. "I promise."

He shook his head and said, "Listen to me first. Then think about what I am going to tell you. Give me your word only after that."

I nodded.

"First of all, I want you to promise me that no one will know the identity of this woman but you."

I nodded again.

"Then you must promise that you will help yourself to emerge from this mess."

With difficulty, I sat up straight and answered him without thinking.

"I promise. I promise."

.11.

On the day we had returned from the central morgue, Saeed and Nargess had picked up Soudabeh and had gone to Amin's office. In front of the door, Soudabeh, with a pale face and trembling lips, was reluctant to go in. Once inside, Saeed had asked her to sit down. Nargess turned her back on them and cried silently. It was a cry she had suppressed for the past week.

"Come here. Let's go through the telephone lists," Saeed said.

Nargess turned around and her eyes caught Soudabeh's bewildered eyes. As she moved, Soudabeh moved too. She went to her desk, opened a drawer, and brought out two slim notebooks, one black and one blue. She gave them to Nargess.

"This one is the list of patients. The other one is the list of doctors, hospitals, and other contacts."

Nargess took the books and sat on one of the chairs. Soudabeh slowly sat next to her. Saeed thought that she was acting like a sleepwalker. Nargess opened the blue notebook, in which there was an alphabetical list of names and phone numbers. She knew none of the names. She looked at Soudabeh, who seemed to be feeling better.

"I think you know these people."

Soudabeh bent over the book and put her fleshy finger on the first name.

"This is the operator of the x-ray department in Jahan Clinic."

"Was he a friend of the doctor?"

"No. I contacted him to make appointments for the patients. This one is the specialist at the lab where the doctor used to send his patients for tests. He always used to talk to him personally."

Saeed, not yet convinced that he would find anything by contacting these people, addressed Soudabeh.

"Soudabeh Khanum, do you think we can get any results by contacting these people? You know them better than we do."

There was a pause. Then Soudabeh asked, "What kind of result do you have in mind?"

Saeed did not answer her question. So, Nargess, still looking at the notebook, began to talk.

"It can't be fruitless. One of these people could have introduced the woman to the doctor. I mean, the woman who had her abortion here."

Soudabeh was silent, with her empty eyes fixed on an unknown point.

"As I think this over and over again, I cannot see the point of this," Saeed said. "You see, Nargess, if these people knew anything and intended to tell us what they knew, they would have come forward and told us during these past few days. And if they thought that they shouldn't tell us anything, then they wouldn't do so even if we contacted them."

Nargess closed the notebook and looked at Saeed.

"Is there anything else we can do?"

Saeed shrugged his shoulders.

"I still think that we should tell the police about this woman. It is no longer important to keep this abortion a secret. In the beginning, we did not want to get Amin in trouble. But now, what is more important, finding him or sticking to this foolish secrecy? Let's assume that we find him and they take away his license. So what? The hell with the license. I say that the police are better equipped to find that woman."

Nargess accepted Saeed's logic but still could not make up her mind. She was looking at Saeed with a confused manner. Saeed began to pace.

"We do not even need to tell Hajji. We can tell the police that the doctor's secretary has just told us the story."

He looked at Soudabeh to get her approval, and saw that her face had turned blue and her eyes had filled with fright. Worried, Saeed moved toward her to put his hand on her shoulder. She drew back like a frightened child.

"No.... Please don't do such a thing. Don't tell the police," she moaned.

Nargess, still sitting next to Soudabeh, turned and faced her.

"Why are you so frightened, Soudabeh? You're not responsible for what happened. They cannot do you any harm."

Saeed completed her thought.

"Soudabeh Khanum, rest assured that this won't harm you at all. The doctor himself is responsible for what happens under this roof. It doesn't relate to you. You could even say that you were not asked to help him in such instances."

Soudabeh had grasped Saeed's hands as if standing on the edge of a deep cliff. With a voice unlike her own, she uttered her words hastily.

"No. No. Please don't do such a thing."

Then she hid her face between her hands and burst into thunderous tears. Nargess and Saeed were caught by surprise. Nargess leaned toward Soudabeh to embrace her, but the secretary withdrew and almost cried out.

"I am the one. I had that abortion. I am the woman you're looking for."

Nargess's arms, still reaching for Soudabeh, froze in mid-air. Saeed slowly sat down and asked, "Why didn't you tell us this before?"

Soudabeh's answer came between her sobs.

"If my brother and mother knew about this, they undoubtedly would kill me. You know? They'd kill me."

Nargess sat motionless with her hands in her lap. She was remembering the words of the man who had called that afternoon. He had told her that Amin was arrested at the end of Alborz Avenue. And Nargess knew that Soudabeh lived just at the end of that road. She put her hand on Soudabeh's shoulder.

"Did Amin take you to your place or did he drop you off at the beginning of Alborz Avenue?"

Soudabeh did not raise her head to look at her.

"I didn't feel well. He took me to my place."

Nargess and Saeed looked at each other. Now they both believed the caller. Saeed felt a narrow line of sweat run down his back. He went to Soudabeh's desk and switched on the fan. At the same time he asked Soudabeh, "But why didn't you tell us this on the first day. Why?"

Soudabeh suddenly sat upright. Her face was swollen and bright red. She looked at Saeed and answered his question with a barely perceptible voice.

"I could not possibly say it. No, I could not. Because the father of my child was Dr. Amin Jalali."

Saeed stared at her. Amin's name escaped Nargess's lips amid a moan and her face dropped onto the cushion. Soudabeh turned toward her and took her arm with both hands. Her voice was soft and impassioned.

"I swear to God that I was not the one who brought this about. Please do not disgrace me. My brother and mother will kill me if they hear about this."

Nargess was leaning back, calm and motionless, with her eyes closed. Saeed tried to pull himself together. He put his hand on Soudabeh's shoulder.

"Don't be afraid, Soudabeh. Nargess and I won't tell anyone. I promise."

Nargess opened her eyes and saw on the wall a picture of a woman nursing her child. Then she gently caressed Soudabeh's hair. Tears rolled down Nargess's cheeks.

Later, she told me that she couldn't understand why she was crying. Was it because she knew that her brother was arrested by Revolutionary Guards? Or was it because she realized that her faith in her brother was waning away?

• • • • •

I parked my car in the narrow alley and made my way through a crowd of women standing on the pavement and wailing as they watched the mourning procession. I moved with difficulty toward Soudabeh's place. Her house was situated next to a humble real estate office. In front of the shop, a man was standing on a stool and pouring rosewater onto the crowd. This was the very spot where Amin had said his last farewell to Soudabeh five months ago. It was the same spot where the Revolutionary Guards had arrested him and taken him away. Some drops of rosewater fell onto my face. I stood in front of Soudabeh's house. I knew the low green door quite well; on a few occasions I had accompanied Amin as he drove Soudabeh home. I looked for the bell but I couldn't find it. Then I saw the black metal knocker in the middle of the door. I knocked. A few long moments passed and there was no answer. The mourning women passed by, jostling and pressing me to the door. The sun had almost reached high noon.

I had telephoned Soudabeh an hour ago. I had not slept the night before. I believed that, unless I talked to Soudabeh, I would not be able to control my nerves, as well as my thirsty curiosity. Soudabeh was surprised by my call and when I said that I needed to see her she had remained silent.

I had explained my reason. "I need to talk to you about the office. I won't take much of your time."

Soudabeh sounded calm. "By all means. Do you want me to come to your place tomorrow?"

I had answered her with haste. "No. I'll come to your place. I'll be there within the hour." Soudabeh had remained silent, so I hung up.

I knocked again. This time the door immediately opened wide and Soudabeh invited me in. I entered a dark, narrow corridor that ended in a yard. An elderly woman was standing in the yard wearing a black veil and looking at us curiously. Before reaching the yard, Soudabeh opened a door and took me into a room.

It was a dark and mildly heated room with simple furniture. The floor was covered by a cheap, red carpet. The comfortable chairs were old and brownish. By the chairs, there was a short rectangular table on which a china vase was filled with artificial flowers. A small kerosene heater in a corner had not been turned on. I sat next to a small window covered by a thick, green curtain. On the opposite wall, a huge, cheap painting displayed a stormy sea. I felt my heart beating like mad. I still did not know what I was going to say to her. Soudabeh came into the room with a tea tray.

"This is a nice room," I said.

She smiled and did not say anything. I took the teacup.

"Have you found a job yet?" I asked.

She put the empty tray in a corner and came to sit across from me. She crossed her legs.

"How on earth can one find a job after this revolution?"

She gazed at me, as if waiting for a suggestion. I looked at her well-shaped legs, which had caught my eye the first day I had met her. I had considered her an attractive girl. Her short hair was arranged nicely and her fleshy body was framed with a well-cut, fashionable dress. Her skin was dark chocolate, as dark as her eyes, which were a nice match for her ever-smiling face. Amin had been quite happy with her work. He had said, "Since Soudabeh has joined the office, the patients don't mind sitting for a while in the waiting room."

She was friendly with the patients and listened to them with attention and care. Nevertheless, Amin often said that he did not like her. On a few occasions, I wanted to invite her to our parties. Amin was always against it. "I don't want her coming and going in our place. I don't approve of the way she behaves. She is too noisy and gay. She is also nosy and wants to know everything about everyone."

Soudabeh was still waiting for me to say what I wanted to say. I thought that her brown eyes were darker than usual. I looked away before speaking.

"Soudabeh, I'm not here to cause you any harm. I am not even angry with you. I'm here just to clear up a few things."

Soudabeh was taken by surprise. She blinked rapidly and leaned forward.

"Yes?"

I gradually realized why I had tried my best to be there at that moment.

"I know everything," I said. Then I lowered my voice.

"I know about your relationship with my husband and that is not important to me any more. But I need to know all the details."

Her mouth was wide open and her pupils shrunk to small dots. I stood up and went to sit on the chair next to her.

"I told you that I won't harm you. Everything is over now."

Her head dropped down and I saw tears falling on her knees. Her voice was weak and shaky.

"What do you want to know? I've told everything to Nargess Khanum and Saeed Agha."

"No. What I want to know is different. You may have told them what I'm looking for. But they haven't related it to me. Could you tell me when your affair with the doctor began?"

Soudabeh hid her face in her hands as she cried softly.

"Please don't cry. Just answer me. Whatever you say won't change anything. But tell me the truth. I need to know the truth."

Soudabeh did not say a word. She stood up and went to the other window, which looked out on the yard. She opened a narrow gap in the thick green curtain and looked out. Then she returned to her chair. Her voice was ridden with sadness.

"My brother will kill me if he finds out about this," she said.

"I promise I won't do you any harm. Amin is the guilty one. Whatever your role was, it is not of any concern to me."

"Ask me. Ask me whatever you want. I won't tell any lies."

Her voice was calm.

"When did this all begin?"

"One month before the revolution."

She suddenly took my hands and moaned.

"Luba Khanum, I swear to God that I didn't start it. Believe me. I didn't start anything."

"I told you that I'm not concerned about that. Don't worry. Just tell me how it began."

Soudabeh grabbed her head and, as if suffering from tremendous pain, her body became taut.

"Sometimes the doctor stayed for a while in the office to talk to me after work. He asked me questions and said sweet things to me. One day he called me to the office and gave me a gold necklace."

She unconsciously moved her hand to her neck and grabbed a gold chain from which two little balls dangled. I remembered that Amin's first present to me was also a necklace — one with two little gold-and-white pigeons. I had been in the hospital for two months before Bardia was born. Afterward, I remained there for a week before Amin came to take me home in an ambulance. Throughout those two months, he came to see me whenever he had a chance during his work at the hospital. When he was on the night shift, he sat next to my bed and talked to me. He was not a stranger anymore. He had turned into a lovable acquaintance whom I trusted. On the day he came to pick me up, he gave me a small box.

"I hope you like it," he said.

I took the box and asked, "What is it?"

"A small present for the birth of your son, who I hope will soon be my own son, too."

Soudabeh moved her hand away from the chain and looked at the carpet.

"Then he told me that he was fond of me. He took me in his arms and kissed me."

Before I could say anything, Amin had taken my hand and kissed it. "Will you marry me Luba?"

Soudabeh was looking at me with frightened eyes.

"I resisted hard. But…. I couldn't help it…. I couldn't. Believe me, Luba Khanum, I didn't want to have such relations with him. Actually, when I came to know that he had relations with that other woman, I was shocked. I felt sorry for you."

"Another woman?"

My voice must have been very loud because Soudabeh jumped and went to look out of the window at the yard. Then she returned and sat opposite me.

"Didn't you know about her?" she said, confused.

I shook my head.

Soudabeh's face had regained its dark chocolate tint and her eyes were deep brown again.

"Do you mean that you didn't know about the relationship he had with Mrs. Dowlatian for years?"

Something like an old metal wheel was loudly whirling in my head — so loudly that I felt Soudabeh was able to hear it.

"Mrs. Dowlatian? Do you mean Eliza?"

I had known Eliza, Dr. Dowlatian's wife, for years. I met the couple in England after my marriage. Dr. Dowlatian was Amin's classmate at the university and had married Eliza a year before. She was a zealous Italian Catholic who attended church every Sunday without fail. Even when we came to Iran, she did not change her church-going habit. They came to Iran one year after us. We were not close friends, so I seldom saw her. We had only met because of our husbands' friendship. Apart from that, we had no common interests. If we had to sit together at a party, we had nothing to talk about but the weather and our children, or the new Persian dishes she had learned to cook.

It seemed to me that Soudabeh had forgotten why I was sitting there. She was clearly enjoying the disclosure of a secret she had found so surprising to me.

"I don't know how many years this relationship had dragged on. But I knew they were friends from the moment I began my work at the office up until the time she left Iran. Of course I became aware of their affair a few months after I started my job."

She was talking nonstop now and went through every detail before I asked any questions. She told me that every week, on Mondays and Thursdays, Eliza used to go to the office, always as the last patient Amin saw at the end of the working day. She would go directly into the examining room.

"I have to stay for an hour. You can go home now," Amin would tell Soudabeh. She did not become suspicious because she initially believed that Eliza needed some kind of medical treatment. As soon as she arrived at the office, Eliza would call her husband to say that she was tied up for an hour and could not come home earlier. In addition, Soudabeh knew that Amin had daily contacts with Dr. Dowlatian and they often sent their patients to one another.

Then, one day, when Soudabeh left the office, she remembered that she had forgotten to pass an urgent message on to Amin. She knocked at the door and entered the examining room. There, she caught them naked. They were so involved in their lovemaking that they were not aware of her presence at first. Soudabeh could have left the room without them noticing, if she had been able to overcome the paralyzing shock she had felt through her body. At last, Eliza saw her, jumped up, and reached for her clothes. Soudabeh regained her control and left without passing on the message she had come to tell Amin. The next day, Amin behaved normally, but Soudabeh was so ashamed that she could not look at his face. The next Thursday, Amin told her to leave the office half an hour earlier. Curious, Soudabeh waited across the street next to a newspaper kiosk. She saw Eliza come out of a taxi and enter the office. "The doctor's wife is younger and more beautiful than Mrs. Dowlatian," she had thought. She was puzzled as to why Amin had kept and continued to hold onto this relationship.

"Where did they make love?" I asked.

"On the examining table."

"Did he sleep with you there as well?"

Soudabeh was taken aback. She suddenly realized that she had done the same thing that she was telling me Eliza had done. She looked away and nodded.

"Did he actually make love to you?" I asked.

Soudabeh looked at me in a confused way. Then she turned her head away hastily. I felt unusually angry and repeated my question in a harsh tone.

"I asked you a question. Did he make love to you or just sleep with you?"

Soudabeh looked at me helplessly. Her face was blue again. At that moment, she did not seem to be a twenty-two-year-old woman. She was like a little girl choking on a big piece of food.

"I don't know, Luba Khanum. I don't understand what you mean. This was the only sexual experience I had had in my life. I have not slept with any other man."

Her broken words and her trembling voice brought me back to my senses. I pitied her for the situation she was in and hated myself. I stood up. Soudabeh had hidden her face in her hands and was crying once more.

"Forget it. Forget what happened today. Just forget everything."

I uttered the words hastily. Then I left the room, walked through the corridor, and let myself out of the green door, into the road.

The chaotic turmoil of people, drums, and cymbals had reached its peak. It was noon on *Ashura*, the tenth day of Moharram. According to Shi'ite mythology, Hossein, the third Imam, was martyred on the stroke of noon, while his family was taken captive. When I reached the main road, the crowd was mourning so feverishly that one would have thought their Imam had been slain only a few moments ago. It was the first *Ashura* after the victory of the revolution; this coincidence contributed to the gravity of the occasion. During the Shah's regime, the processions were only allowed to take place in certain areas of the city.

Dazed, I walked through the crowd and finally reached my car. The roads were half-closed and traffic moved very slowly. I drove through a background of noise and a rapid sequence of faded faces belonging to those who had played roles in my past life: my mother, Amin, my father, Soudabeh, Amin, Julia, my mother, Amin, Stella, Bardia, Milan, Saeed, Nargess, Amin, Hajji, my mother, Eliza, Bahram, Amin.... They each appeared in a flash and were then replaced by other images.

Now that I look back on those moments, they seem like an unreal part of my life, like a disturbed and confused dream, filled with people and things that take other forms in reality.

.12.

Bewildered, Fatemeh Khanum watched me as I stood motionless in the middle of the room.

"Luba Khanum, why are you standing here? Do you want me to bring you a cup of tea?" she asked.

She was an interesting, lively, and agile woman. During the six years she had worked for us, I had never seen her in a bad mood. She had lost her husband when she was very young, and had worked ever since in order to raise her son and daughter. Her children were now grown up and had their own jobs. They were capable of helping their mother with her expenses, but she had refused to be helped by anyone. Her own busywork was the meaning of her life and she liked it that way.

When she realized that I had not heard her, she repeated her question.

"Luba Khanum, can I be of any help?"

I did not know what I wanted to do. The apartment seemed ugly and unbearable. Nothing was in its proper place. The arrangement of the furniture had to be changed. The dining room table had to be closer to the window. The small table with the lampshade had to be moved away from the window to some other corner of the room.... The kitchen had to be rearranged.... The bedroom, too....

When Ahmad knocked on the front door, I was still standing motionless in the middle of the room. I recognized his knock. It was like a cat batting the door gently with his paws and waiting for an answer. When he entered, I noticed his bright grayish eyes were as happy as a summer morning.

"Hey there! Why are you standing here? Anything wrong?" he asked.

I looked at him. Since his relationship with Nargess had started, he had become so joyful and relaxed. He continued.

"Nargess just called to see how you were. She said she already talked to Fatemeh Khanum, who said she didn't see you at home when she had arrived. Nargess said that they have been waiting to see you at Hajji's. For the *Ashura* lunch."

"I was out. I had to attend to some things. I'll call them. I can't go there today. This place needs a lot of attention."

I started like a bulldozer.

Ahmad later told Nargess about what we did that day. "We had the whole apartment in a state of disarray in a few seconds. Luba was in a strange mood. But there was nothing to worry about. She acted comfortably and with precision. She moved the tables around. The table in the kitchen was moved nearer to the balcony. All of the flowerpots were taken from the kitchen and the balcony and put into other rooms. She separated the beds and put one of them outside the apartment and the other one under the window. She put a few of the flowerpots in the bedroom and said it was foolish to think that flowers would crowd the bedroom. She took every photo of herself and Amin from the bedroom and living room. But she didn't touch the ones in the children's rooms. She didn't change anything in those rooms. She emptied the closets and separated Amin's clothes and personal belongings. She packed them in a black suitcase, which she put outside the front door. She laughingly asked Fatemeh Khanum to find someone to take the items. Fatemeh Khanum asked where she wanted them to be taken and Luba answered that she could take them anywhere and give them to anyone she liked. She also had permission to dispose of them if she couldn't find anyone to take them. She said she would pay the expenses if needed. Once the changes were complete, she threw herself into a chair and said, 'Now one can light a cigarette and drink a cup of tea!'"

When Fatemeh Khanum and Ahmad were gone, I covered the kitchen table — now in the place I had wished it to be for seven years — with all sorts of food, as if I were expecting guests. I put the vodka bottle in front of me and began drinking with sheer relief. I felt strangely happy, unaffected even by the faraway sad voices of the mourners, who were then recreating the first night of their Imam's family in captivity. On that night, "The Night of the Strangers," Shi'ites light candles and turn off the other lights in order to mourn that sacred family late into the night.

I drank vodka and was happy with the way my home had been transformed. Everything had been put in locations of which Amin would not have approved. But Amin himself was still there, behind the kitchen window, standing on the balcony, and watching the mourning night. His head was large and loomed over the whole city.

My father, who was leaning against the window frame, said, "They're now igniting the fuses they've installed in the tunnel under the statue. 1,450 fuses. It's not a joke!"

Stursa, my father's close friend, standing next to him, said, "We'll see the fireworks of 800 kilos of explosives. 800 kilos!"

My mother, lying next to me on the bed, said, with a voice that rose from the depths of the earth, "Now I'm sure they'll let me sing."

The series of explosions began that very moment. The first one lit the whole city. Then the whirling tubes of bluish smoke rose up from the Lechna Heights toward the sky. With each explosion, I could imagine the fall of one statue — that of a worker, a botanist, a female hero, a soldier of the Red Army. The biggest explosion was saved for Stalin himself. His tall body fell with a shock. Suddenly, the ground itself rolled into a whirlwind and rose up toward the sky....

My mother was looking at the window, the panes of which my father had fixed beforehand with wide, black tape. Then she jumped out of the bed in a state of confusion. Her thin body staggered toward the mirror and sat in front of it before my father could notice. With trembling fingers, she combed her golden hair, the last holdover of the unrivaled beauty of her youth, and said, "I have to make up my face. I cannot appear in front of the crowd in such a mess."

My father took her arms, and led her back to bed. "If you want to be able to sing again, you have to become healthy first. You have to help yourself to become strong again."

My mother's lips formed the shade of a smile on her stark white face. "Who can believe that he's dead?" she said.

I, too, could not believe it. How could that huge monument, which had grown out of the stones of the hilltops overlooking the river, to keep a constant watch on our lives, be destroyed? No. He was not dead. He was sitting there on the balcony rail with his blue-striped shirt and gray trousers, laughing at me with a kind of laughter I didn't like, a teasing laughter that poured out of his slightly slanted lips whenever he ridiculed others. My mother was looking at me from the bed; her fingers trembled like thin, fragile vegetable shoots in a strong wind. Unlike other instances, I didn't feel like crying as I always did when I saw those withered hands. I did not wish that all the winds of the earth would stop. I was full of wrath and the warm, slimy anger perched on my back and tore my skin apart to penetrate into my veins. I felt like I was being choked. And he was still standing on the balcony, laughing at me. I moved toward him. My father and Stursa were gazing at the square, looking in bewilderment at his head, which was still supported proudly on a thin metallic blade. There was nothing left of the bluish dust but a mist of brittle particles on the Vancess Las Square. My mother stood up and ran toward the window. I heard her shouting, "His head! I have to get rid of his head." Before anybody could do anything, she opened the window, the cool breeze of the autumn night covering her skin. She took a long breath and she saw him once again, sitting on the balcony rail, with his back to the Alborz Mountains and his wide shoulders hiding the mourning city. She moved toward him. She now knew that she had to finish him off, she had to throw him down from the balcony and watch him break into pieces. And she flew....

Saeed had been at Ahmad's apartment since early that evening. He had thought that with Nargess's help he could see me. But she had told him, "Luba wished to be left alone. Why should we bother her?" Although Saeed had not detected anything wrong in my voice on the telephone, and despite the fact that Ahmad had told him I was fine, he had not been able to wait for more than two hours.

"We shouldn't leave her alone tonight," he said. All three of them came to see me. They knocked at the door several times but did not receive any answer. Nargess ran to get her purse from the car and opened the front door with her key. She ran toward the bedroom but, seeing my shadow on the edge of the balcony, she shouted aloud.... The two men were quick enough to grab me just in time.

• • • • •

I was in the hospital for a week. Now I can only recall the last two days of that period. During the first few days, still in a state of semi-consciousness, I occasionally opened my eyes and saw Nargess, Soraya, Saeed, and others from behind a curtain of moonlit dust. Sometimes I could hear familiar voices. I tried to move my eyelids but I could only see a huge white ceiling, hanging high over me.

The first day that I could see the others, I found Nargess by my side. She was standing next to a metal rod that bore the weight of a fluid bag connected to my arm through a long transparent plastic tube. She was looking at me with those large eyes, glowing like two bright pearls. I smiled at her.

"I'm very hungry," I said.

Her lips opened in a joyful smile.

"Just wait," she said.

She went away. When my eyes followed her, I could see the rest of the room. It was a clean and cozy room, fully equipped with all of the medical accessories that one could find in the luxurious private hospitals of Tehran. A few moments later, she returned with a young nurse. The nurse put her hand on my forehead and asked how I felt. Then she checked my blood pressure and spoke to me in a gentle voice.

"They'll bring your food shortly."

One hour later, Soraya came to see me. She explained that they had not been able to drag me out of semi-consciousness for a few days. With my very low blood pressure and my irregular heartbeat, they were worried about me, but had pinned their hopes on my physical strength.

Soraya wanted to help me do something about my severe depression. But I was quite all right. I felt a deep kind of joy in my whole body. I felt like someone coming out of a serious car crash without any serious injury. I told Soraya about the way I felt.

"Sometimes these are good signs indicating that the crisis is over. But sometimes they could be the signal of the beginning of a more severe one."

She recommended that I stay in the hospital for two more weeks. But, since I was only slightly weak, I persistently asked her to let me go home. She helplessly looked at Nargess.

"I won't take any responsibility. Luba has to stay in the hospital for two more weeks or she should be transferred to somewhere other than her own home. And someone should always keep an eye on her," she said.

Nargess suggested that after a few more days we should all go to Golsara so that I could rest there for a couple of days. Soraya liked the idea but I disagreed. I was worried about the children and missed them very much. Bahram, Hajji, and Esmat Khanum, who, besides some occasions like birthdays, had seldom come to our place, had repeatedly visited me in the hospital. But Nargess informed me that Bardia had only come once. When I regained full consciousness and was in the hospital for three more days, he came to see me just one more time.

He had a frazzled appearance, as if he just returned from a long, tiresome trip. When I asked him why he didn't come to see me more often, he looked out of the window.

"I don't have time. Every day we go to the embassy with our teachers. At night, I have to go to the mosque," he said.

I was furious again. I asked him angrily if he had any other things to do, any kind of homework. He looked at me in a way I had never seen before. Then he turned away.

"To me, Islamic and revolutionary duties are much more important than anything else."

I did not know what to say. Soraya, who was standing next to me, feared I might say something which would add to the gravity of the situation. She interrupted our conversation.

"This is not a suitable time for this kind of discussion. It's better to postpone it until you return home."

Once Bardia left the room, she told me that, until I had regained control, I should not go home or engage in any kind of discussions with Bardia.

"He is in a situation that demands a lot of patience and tolerance from you if you want to help change him for the better."

.13.

Hajji's childhood home, Golsara (the House of Flowers), was located between Nowshahr and Shahsavar, by the Caspian Sea. It had a large garden with a huge number of orange trees. The building was more than 100 hundred years old. Whenever I entered Golsara, it created a sense of ecstasy and tranquility in me. Golsara and its five huge rice silos, were the remainders of an exorbitant inheritance Hajji had received from his father, Mohammad Khan. Hajji had sold the rest of his father's property once he decided to move to the capital, Tehran. He had built a mosque, called Mohammad, in Tehran and had started his trading career in the bazaar with the rest of his money. He needed the rice silos because he was mainly involved in the rice trade. He said he had kept Golsara as a token of his father's memory.

I had been there with Nargess and the children several times in the summer. Amin seldom joined us. He did not like Golsara; he believed it should be knocked down so that a new building could be constructed in its place. But I dearly loved its old originality. Golsara had its own special identity. The tall walls with huge wooden doors and windows, all bearing decorative spikes, were rather similar to a castle. The two-story thatched-roof house had a large balcony covered with green stones and sheltered by a carefully arranged cane roof. The balcony faced the sea and had a flight of wide stairs that led to a sandy beach. There were eleven rooms in the house, six of which had windows that opened toward the sea. The largest room, as large as a parlor, had a huge door that opened onto the balcony.

This central room was the gathering place for the members of the family who went to Golsara during the summer. Its floor was covered by three large uniform carpets ornamented with a detailed green design. The dining table and its twelve chairs, made of precious local wood, were in a corner of the room. The rest of the room was filled with numerous colorful cushions used as back rests. The tall ceiling was decorated with plaster moldings and the four large windows, which opened onto the garden and the sea, were inserted in the wide white walls like four lively, bright picture frames.

On one side of the room, a huge fireplace displayed on its stone mantelpiece a collection of copper and bronze pieces, as well as chinaware that was rarely used. On the same wall, a black-and-white framed picture of Mohammad Khan, showing his joined eyebrows and his young keen eyes, was surrounded by eight large white-and-gold silk flowers. The picture showed the young Mohammad Khan in his twenties.

It was early evening when Nargess, Saeed, Ahmad, and I arrived. Although it was an autumn evening, the weather was as warm and calm as if it were summer. Jawaher and Musa, the couple who took care of the house, welcomed us. The last time I had seen them was during the mourning ceremonies for Amin. Later on, I was told that Nargess previously had warned them not to mention anything related to recent events. So they already knew that we were coming and, as usual, had turned on all the lights. The house was filled with the delicious smells of local food and fish kabobs. In a corner of the central room, water boiled in a huge coal-lit samovar. The fragrance of wild rue strewn on the coals lurked mysteriously throughout the house.

After a few tense months, I was suddenly feeling happy. For a while, I stood on the very spot of the balcony where Amin used to stand and watch the sea. I leaned on its wooden fence and thought about Amin only for a brief moment. Nevertheless, Nargess was watchful. She did not let me stay there alone.

"While we're here, you shouldn't leave me alone. You shouldn't be alone either," she said.

She was her usual giddy self and the aura of her joyful presence spread through the air, attracting everyone to her. Saeed and Ahmad, who were spending the weekend with us, were absorbed in their backgammon game. I had learned the game in Iran and could play it with skill. What I lacked was the joyful technique of boasting and bragging; Iranians used every psychological trick to discourage their opponents throughout the game. I laughed a lot at the players' inventions and slanders; I enjoyed listening to the comical words they used to belittle each other.

We were engaged in the game until late at night. When I finally went to bed, I immediately fell asleep and enjoyed nine hours of rest without the aid of alcohol or tranquilizers. It seemed to be the end of those long months of insomnia.

● ● ● ● ●

The sound of the waves woke me up in the morning. They sounded louder than they had the previous night. I took a shower in the bathroom, which was the only modern room in the house. Then, feeling energetic and delighted, I went into the living room. No one was there. The room was as clean and organized as it had been the moment we arrived. I could find no one on the balcony either. I heard Jawaher and Musa talking loudly in the local dialect of Northern Iranians; their voices filtered from the kitchen window under the balcony. I decided to go there and make myself a cup of coffee. But Saeed entered the balcony with a colorful breakfast tray.

"It seems that you slept well," he said.

The morning light had darkened his brown eyes. They seemed so gentle under the shadow of his eyelashes.

"I couldn't have slept better," I said.

We sat on the wooden chairs and watched the autumn sea.

"Where are Nargess and Ahmad?" I asked.

"They went to Nowshahr to do some shopping."

Then he dragged his chair close to mine.

"I am supposed to sit here and see that you finish your breakfast."

I looked at the tray. The breakfast was more than enough for two people. I laughed. "Do you want me to eat this much?"

Saeed caressed his mustache. "No. This is not just for you. I'll have some, too."

But when I began to eat, he leaned back on his chair and, while talking to me, gazed at the waves. Tall and proud, the waves rushed forward so that their majestic shadows covered the sands. Then, on their way back, as if breathless and exhausted, they struck the turbulent surface of the sea, which opened its arms and invited them inside. There was no resistance left in the waves. They jumped into that welcoming breast and faded away… away… away….

Saeed was telling me about a new book he had received from England and finished the night before. It was Rosa Luxembourg's *Letters to a Comrade and Lover*, published years after it had been banned. Its English translation was only recently available.

Saeed knew some parts of one of the letters by heart. He recited them for me. I could see that he still had a lot of sensitivity and emotion. Fourteen years before, when he was in his early twenties, he had been fully charged with such passion. Although his many years of political activity had deepened his mind and insight, it had not lessened the delicacies of his soul.

"Could we go for a walk, or are you supposed to keep me from moving?"

He laughed.

"I don't think taking a walk could do any harm."

We went down the stairs toward the sea. But as soon as I set foot on the sand, Amin told me, "You should take your shoes off. You'll see how nice it is." I never liked to take them off but, as usual, I could not refuse him. He did not like negative responses. I took my shoes off and picked them up. Amin, as usual, tried to take them from me and put them down. "Don't worry. No one will take them." I stood motionless and looked away from Amin.

"Why did you take your shoes off? Don't you think your feet might get hurt?" Saeed asked inquisitively.

I happily put them on again and took Saeed's arm.

"Let's go back. I don't think I have enough strength for a walk," I said.

● ● ● ● ●

After a pleasant day, we began the second night of our stay in Golsara. Throughout the day, there had been no mention of political issues and the miseries overshadowing the lives of Iranians outside of our sheltered world. Only in the way others talked and behaved did I realize how grave my condition had been. I could see that they all had agreed to whisk me from the real world into a secluded, beautiful one full of nothing but sheer tranquility so that I could regain my lost strength.

Once they had finished their duties, Jawaher and Musa had gone to their home on the other side of the garden to go to bed early, as all rustic people usually do. We were left alone with the sea and the night. The waves, singing their softest songs, had invited us to the balcony. We sat there in silence and watched our host.

The autumn night was not cold. The sky was cloudless and the sea was tame. Little waves moved lazily toward the seaside and, once on their way back under the moonlight, turned into thousands of pearls returning to the accepting sea. We could hear the seagulls, whose sounds resembled the music of a primitive world. A gentle breeze passed over the sea to spread the aroma of orange blossoms.

Saeed sat across from me. Whenever I looked at him, his eyes were filled with a dauntless desire that made me rejoice with a youth thought lost but now regained. I had returned to those days when Saeed would come to my place every night. It was a small room, with my bed in one corner and a gas stove in the other. I had a small table and just one chair.

"Sit on the bed," he would tell me. He set up a cushion as a back rest for me and dragged the table as near to the bed as he could. Then he emptied the bags he had brought and began cooking. He usually cooked Iranian food which, despite its strangeness, had a pleasant smell and taste. We would eat together. He sat there on the chair and waited until I fell asleep. Then, when I woke up in the morning, I would notice that he had washed the dishes, organized the room, and gone back to his own home. Most nights, he played a record he had given to me as a present during the early days of our acquaintance. It was one of my mother's records. The small turntable was a gift from him, as well. My mother sang for us and for Bardia, who listened to her with his invisible ears inside my womb. It was like a sweet lullaby that took Bardia and me away, into the realm of sweet dreams.

I suddenly stood up.

"I want to play a record I like for Saeed."

There was a gentle glitter in Nargess's eyes. Without a word she looked at me and Saeed with a naughty expression. Without looking at Saeed, I went to my room to fetch a tape Saeed had made from that record years ago. I had put it in my suitcase while hastily preparing for the trip. I returned to the balcony with the tape. Nargess had already set up the tape recorder.

Like a chandelier dancing with its hundreds of little shiny crystal pendants amid the sounds of the tide, Marta's voice began swinging in the air.

Saeed, recognizing Marta's voice, leaned back and plunged into thoughts I deeply wished to know. Ahmad and Nargess attentively listened to a song that they had never heard before.

When Marta's voice faded away and the waves and gulls returned to the balcony, Ahmad was the first one to speak.

"What a voice. Although I couldn't understand one word of what she sang, it was as if she was singing a piece of poetry in my language. I could feel all of the emotions." Then he looked at me.

"Who is she, Luba?"

Saeed raised his head, looked at me gratefully, and answered.

"It's Marta. Luba's mother…."

Nargess was excited and reproachful.

"Luba! You hadn't told us anything about her before…."

I did not tell her how Amin had resented anything belonging to my past, including my mother's voice.

"It makes me sad. But tonight I knew that I wouldn't be sad," I said.

"Do you have any other work of hers?" Ahmad asked.

"No. This one is from a record Saeed found for me in London."

Saeed began to talk about Marta with excitement. His information was based on what I had told him and what he had read on the cover of the record. I was amazed at how he could remember every detail.

"Was she alive when you came out of your country?"

Again, it was Saeed who answered.

"No. She died years before."

Then he smartly changed the subject.

"This song won the Nightingale Prize, which is the most prestigious artistic award in Czechoslovakia. She won this prize for three consecutive years. I was so sorry that I couldn't find the other two songs."

Nargess rewound the tape.

"I want to hear it once more," she said.

And Marta began to sing again:

> *I smell the scent of flight*
> *From the wings of a bird*
> *Caught in a cage.*
>
> *O, you, bird*
> *That flies above my head*
> *Passing through the blue sky*
> *You are accustomed to your flight*
> *And, thus, you've forgotten it…*
>
> *Come with me*
> *For a moment to this cage…*
>
> *Just for a moment.*
> *A brief moment.*

My braided hair was tied in a long white ribbon that poured down my shoulders. I was sitting next to my father in the first row, trembling amid the explosion of applause. The large hall was shaking ceaselessly and everyone was shouting, "Marta… Marta…" Marta, in her long pink dress, was standing on the stage with her honey-brown eyes filled with joy. Her hands were raised in the air and she looked at the audience with proud, gentle smiles. I wished she would look at me too. Only at me. But her eyes were indifferent. Her glance paused on me as much as it did on others. It was after that night that they took her away.

A few months later, when she came back, there was no glitter in her eyes and no smile on her lips. She was not allowed to sing anymore. She could not find any other job. Well, not exactly. She found a job in a toy factory that made doll bodies. She was to make headless toys. The heads were made in another factory. She could not tolerate it for more than eighteen months and eventually was taken to a mental hospital. After that she was housebound and would never know that Jerry Cerny, the famous music critic, had called her voice "a dancing crystal chandelier." She never knew that throughout the time she constructed headless dolls, or lay in the hospital, or stared out of her window at the huge Stalin monument smiling proudly at her from the Lechna Heights, people sang her songs in private and kept her name alive in their memory.

Saeed took my arms and shook me.

"Don't go anywhere without us."

I looked at him. He was sitting on the arm of my chair. I leaned my head on his shoulder.

"I'm all right. Don't worry."

Nargess stood up and took Ahmad's hand, leading him towards the stairs.

"We'd better go for a walk."

Saeed and I did not move. They went down the stairs toward the sea. The sandy beach under the moonlight stretched out to eternity. It looked like a silky path hiding mysterious bodies and shapes in every corner. Nargess's and Ahmad's shadows followed them, restless and playful. Saeed stood up, just at the moment that I realized I could feel the warmth of his body. He sat next to me, where Nargess was sitting a moment ago.

"Why did you move?" I asked.

With his eyes full of a burning desire, Saeed looked at me.

"I thought you'd be more comfortable this way.'

I stood up and went toward my room.

"Let's go in. I feel cold here," I said.

I walked through the living room and, without looking back, went into my room. A few moments later, Saeed was standing on the threshold. With his long forehead and his prominent nose, he looked like the Achæmenid soldier who had brought the decree of freedom for the Babylonian Jews. As if caught in the instant of puberty, I passed through colorful dandelions and kites and galloped toward those hot springs that can lead you to thirst and satiation at the same time. Saeed came in and we twisted around each other. I fell into a spring and called him to follow me. And he followed… and followed… and followed, and there was no end to it.

• • • • •

When I opened my eyes, morning had settled. My bed still smelled like Saeed. I could not remember when I had fallen asleep or when he had gone. The only thing I could recall was his asking, "Do you want me to stay here tonight?" I had said, "No."

I didn't like the idea of others knowing we had slept together all night. It wasn't that I felt shy or ashamed, but living in Iran, with its traditional family values, had had its impact on me. I knew that there were many reservations about the relations between a man and a woman in that country. If they had enough courage, people could talk about their feelings. But being in love and having an affair with someone and then talking about it was something else. Almost all classical Persian poetry is about love and the human desire for unification with the beloved. The poems tell the amazing stories of unfulfilled love in an atmosphere of melancholic human deprivation. The union of lovers is something that either does not happen or, if it is suggested at all, has no other end but shame and disgrace. Everyone in the country knows these poems by heart; even the very zealous men and women. In their interpretations, however, such love is for God, the eternal beloved of mystics. The desire for unification is nothing but the human hope to return to one's creator. On many religious occasions at Hajji's house, I had noticed that even the most frank erotic poems, veiled in such plausible interpretations, were allowed to penetrate into the most traditional ceremonies of worship.

The more dauntless youngsters could talk about their loves only to their closest friends with utmost secrecy. They made sure that no one else knew if they were involved in love affairs. Of course, men felt quite free to talk about their sexual relations with a woman or a number of women. But this was only when they were either not in love with the woman or had not married her. Marriage wrapped loving relations between husband and wife in a mantle of secrecy. In fact, secrecy was the means by which a marriage became sanctified. Although everyone knew that they went to one another's bed and had intercourse, no one was allowed to talk about such matters. Women were supposed to refrain from talking about their relations both inside the marriage bond and outside of it.

Although Nargess was a liberated woman who had rejected many of her family's traditions, she had not yet discussed her sexual relations with Ahmad and did not intend to do so before anything became serious. But others were aware that they were in love. Even in front of Saeed and me, who knew about her sexual relations with Ahmad, she never touched her lover. Throughout the twenty-four hours that we had spent at the shore, the couple walked and talked together and looked at each other with desire, but I had never seen them go into a room together.

I found Nargess reading a book in the living room. She closed the book when I entered and apologized for having left us the night before. She had not expected us to go to bed so soon. From what she told me, she and Ahmad had found Saeed on the balcony once they had returned from their evening walk along the shore. He had told them that I had just gone to bed.

Saeed and Ahmad had returned to Tehran. Nargess had seen them before they left.

"They left very early in the morning. They wanted to get to work on time."

Then she gave me an envelope.

"Saeed asked me to give you this."

I opened the envelope. It was a short note in English: "You were, you are, and you will be…. See you tomorrow night. Saeed."

I felt blood rushing toward my face. I felt like a young girl. I put the letter back in the envelope.

"He is coming back tomorrow night."

Nargess laughed. I sensed a certain hesitance in her voice when she spoke.

"He can't wait for the weekend. There is no patience in love."

Then, trying not to annoy me, she looked away and stood up.

"I'll go get breakfast."

That day, I told Nargess that I had slept with Saeed. We were leaning on the cushions and I was looking at the silk flowers surrounding Mohammad Khan's picture. Nargess listened to me with excitement.

"Oh my God! So you love him too?'

I nodded. I realized that she could not imagine a man and a woman sleeping together without loving each other. Perhaps, like most of her country people, she believed that sex was a male domain. Only men were allowed to sleep with women without being in love with them. Women were not capable of even thinking of the possibility of such pleasures. So, I did not tell her that the previous night, when I went to bed with Saeed, I did not know if I loved him so much. I made love to him because I wanted to. I wanted to go to bed with him because I decided to experience the act of choosing my own mate. And I had attained an unprecedented pride in doing so.

When we returned to Tehran, after two weeks of living apart from the outside world, I had regained my health and energy. I felt that I was to begin a new life with my thoughts organized and my mind functioning properly.

During those two weeks, Nargess and Saeed had done their best to take me out of the dead and lamenting world in which I had been entrapped into a world full of light and hope. I could see how my lost powers of control were returning to me. I was gradually growing ready to face a new life.

I spent most of the days having long conversations with Nargess. As I got to know her better and more intimately, I saw that her inner world of delicate sensitivities resembled a tender ball of fire. Although she was six years younger than me, her understanding of the world and her keen insight for life was much more mature than mine. I envied her and learned from her, although I wasn't sure that the knowledge I gained in this way could possibly take me to her higher level of existence.

Every night I had long telephone conversations with Esmat Khanum and Bahram; rarely did Bardia get on the phone. After that, Saeed would arrive from Tehran. He drove three hours on a mountainous highway to join me. When Saeed arrived, Nargess would disappear. She would take Ahmad with her if he had accompanied Saeed.

Saeed and I decided to see each other secretly in Tehran. We wanted to keep our relationship as secret as possible and only as long as Amin's parents could accept that their daughter-in-law was entitled to enjoy her life, too. We both knew that in Iran a woman was not supposed to have a relationship with another man shortly after her husband's death; particularly if this husband was considered a martyr.

Nevertheless, neither of us could know of the many other things awaiting us in Tehran which would make it impossible for us to see each other, even briefly.

.14.

The day after I arrived in Tehran, I went to Hajji's place to take the children back home. Bardia, though he had known I was coming, was not there. I asked Esmat Khanum to tell him that I expected him to be home very soon. Esmat Khanum, who had so many untold words in her eyes, nodded.

But the next day, Nargess came to tell me that Bardia had decided to stay at Hajji's place. He had not accepted his grandparents' insistence that he should return home.

"He says that you drink alcohol and do not say your daily prayers," Nargess added. "He does not want to live in the same house as you." Nargess was worried and anxious. "He is not on good terms with me either. Although he pays verbal homage to my parents, I think the only people whom he obeys are his teacher and his schoolmaster."

I asked Saeed and Soraya to help me find a solution for this grave problem. Soraya was even more worried than me.

"I have seen so many youngsters who have adopted deep religious sentiments and have resisted their parents' will accordingly. Such confrontations usually lead children to leave their families for good."

She believed that Bardia was a precarious case because he had lost his beloved father. The anti-religion factions had killed him and the religious zealots considered him a martyr of their revolution. She insisted that I be very careful not to bring about a grave confrontation.

"If you put him under more pressure, he might even leave Hajji's house. He should come to realize that you love him with all your heart."

She recommended that I convince Bardia with sweet talk to come back home. Then I would have a real chance to change his mind.

"Don't forget that he needs a lot of love and care right now."

Nargess, on the contrary, believed that Bardia was not going to return home even if I threw myself at his feet.

"He only listens to his headmaster and teacher," she said.

Thinking of confronting the headmaster once again made me feel sick and I knew that I was not strong enough to look at his black eyes and his chalky face.

"I can't visit the headmaster. And I don't know his teacher. But I'm sure that he is worse than the other."

Saeed, who had remained silent during this discussion, decided to tell us his opinion.

"Even if you could talk to them, you would not get any results. I think that the best solution is to ask Hajji Agha. He can talk to them and they will not give him negative answers."

Both Soraya and Nargess agreed, so I went to see Hajji immediately.

It was a rainy afternoon. The young boys who sold newspapers in the streets were announcing the detention of ten people who had registered as candidates for the first Iranian presidential election in the new republic. The bold letters on the front page of the evening papers displayed the last communiqué of the Student Followers of the Imam inside the American Embassy. The Followers denounced most of the candidates as agents of The Great Satan. As I entered his house, Hajji threw the paper aside and looked at me.

"Now, when they want to eliminate someone, they find some document from inside the American embassy to incriminate him. No one knows how many of these so-called documents they can produce and when they are going to finish."

Because of the takeover and the resignation of the transitional ministers, Hajji was very anxious about the future of his country. He was using his influence to help Bani-Sadr, one of the candidates for the presidency. He believed that Bani-Sadr was Iran's only chance to overcome the chaos, which was spreading quickly like a fatal disease. That afternoon, he lectured me about Bani-Sadr's religious upbringing and his capabilities as a reliable statesman.

"If anyone else is elected, we will see bloodshed all over the country. He is the only one who can put a stop to the advancement of the Communists and prevent these naive children from traveling a path that will end in nothing but their own annihilation."

I had learned from Nargess to listen to him in silence without offering my own opinions. I was waiting for a proper moment to tell him about my problems with Bardia. I knew that Hajji did not approve of what Bardia was doing and was amazed by his sudden changes. He would say regretfully, "I don't know what has made these youngsters so impudent that they can justify their behavior on religious grounds."

At the beginning, Hajji was actually delighted that Bardia was interested in religious beliefs and was curious to know more about Islam. Hajji believed that his religious inclinations could compensate for the loss of his father. He believed that religion could help anyone to forget about his misery and pain. Once he referred to my own situation, which he considered to be the result of Amin's death. He told me, "You know, Luba dear, you're just like my daughter. I don't intend to advise you on what you're doing, but had you given your heart to God and relied on his mercy after your husband's death, you would be a lot better off. A human being is like a small ship caught in the stormy waters of this world. The fate of the ship is in the hands of the captain, God. One should rely on his wise guidance." Nevertheless, when Bardia confined his soul to God — not to receive the comfort he so badly needed, but to join himself with a source of omnipotence that could give him extreme powers — Hajji was furious. "Of course God is omnipotent. Of course he is the ultimate avenger. But these are only two of his attributes. Bardia, along with so many other youngsters, behaves as if the Almighty is summed up by only these two traits."

That day, Hajji also talked about Bardia's bad temper and his bullying of others. He believed that Bardia, and other children like him, interpreted Islam as a religion of fighting with non-believers, rather than as a religion of generosity and the obeying of God's will.

It was only at the end of his long outburst that I could tell him why I was there. He listened to me and kindly accepted my wishes.

"I quite agree with you. I'll do whatever you want me to do. Perhaps, with God's help, your motherly love could give Bardia some peace of mind."

The next day, Hajji went to see the Minister of Education, who, upon Hajji's request, ordered Bardia's teachers and the headmaster to force him to return home. They had told Bardia, "It is your religious duty to supervise the affairs of your mother and brother in the absence of your father." They could have told him many other things as well, things that people traditionally repeat about the importance of the motherhood, but they didn't.

• • • • •

At the end of December, after a few anxious days, Bardia returned home with all of his belongings, which he had gradually transferred to Hajji's house. When I saw him at the door, there was clearly kindness and love in his eyes. He looked exactly like his father, Milan. I took him in my arms after so many months and immediately noticed that he was now taller than me and he had grown larger and stronger. His head, as if too heavy for his neck, leaned slightly toward his shoulder. There was a silent smile on his lips.

I wanted to take his suitcase but he did not let me. He went straight to his room. His smooth, auburn hair, cut in a short military style, seemed much lighter under the golden rays of the evening sun.

While he was carefully taking his shirts from his suitcase and hanging them in the closet with his usual scrupulousness, I began to talk in English. I always felt more comfortable with that language.

"I have suffered so much during the past few months. It is only now that I can recognize how ignorant I have been toward you and your brother. What I wish now is to return to what we were before. We should spend more time together."

While he was hanging one of his shirts, Bardia answered me in Persian.

"I don't want you to drink alcohol any more."

"Sure, my dearest, sure. I was caught in a very bad situation. Your father's death came as a shock to me. You can understand this. You know that...."

I could not end my sentence by saying, "... we had loved each other so much." I could not say such a lie. Bardia turned around, smiled, and looked at me with the honey-colored eyes that resembled my own.

"Did you know that they're taking us to a camp in Khuzistan?"

Last summer his school had also sent their students to a camp on a shore in the north of Iran.

"Is that for the spring or summer holidays?"

Bardia laughed with a childish gesture that made him look as he did before Amin's death.

"No. In one and a half months. For the anniversary of the revolution."

"Are they going to close the schools for the occasion?"

"No, schools will remain opened. They've selected twenty students from each school to receive guerrilla training for a month."

"Guerrilla training?"

I spoke in a protesting voice and suddenly remembered what Soraya had told me. I was not to enter into any arguments with him. So I changed the tone of my voice.

"But aren't you supposed to have your exams in March? Don't you think that being absent from classes will make your exams difficult?"

His tone was very serious.

"No. I won't lose anything. We'll have classes at the camp as well. Besides, this is an order from the Imam…. Anything else is trivial."

I tried to change the subject by motioning to his other suitcase, which he had not yet opened.

"You put your suits in the closets, I'll do the rest."

I opened the suitcase. It was the very one I packed again a month later for his departure for the camp. I was not anxious anymore.

Through that month and a half, I came to realize that there wasn't anything worth worrying about. I felt that Soraya and Nargess were wrong to have alarmed me. I told myself that Bardia had not changed that much at all. He was still my sweet little boy and nothing else. I considered his minor changes as outcomes of puberty. Sometimes he was in a bad mood, sometimes he bullied his brother, sometimes he wanted to establish that he, rather than me, was the head of the family. In such instances, I tried either to be as gentle as I could, or to ignore him. I truly believed that he needed my love and attention. I had not set foot out of the house for the entire period. Upon my return to Tehran, I had requested a leave of absence from the museum for six months so that I could be with the children as much as possible. Even on Thursdays, I preferred to take them to Hajji's place myself. On Friday mornings, Bardia went to the mosque and returned to his grandparents' house, always accompanied by a few new friends whom I did not know. They would go to Amin's old room, which was now Bardia's room, and did not come out at all. Even their lunch was taken to the room.

• • • • •

It was at Hajji's house that I could see Saeed, as well. I looked at him with regret and he watched me reproachfully. I had seen him at his place only once.

He had moved since Margaret had left. He now lived in an apartment near Vanak Square, which was considered to be a fashionable area in the Shah's time. His apartment was in a three-story building at the end of an alley.

It was the first time I had visited him. The apartment was decorated with simple, colorful furniture and did not even remotely resemble his former house. I sat on the only sofa in the living room and looked at him.

"How tranquil this place is."

Saeed sat down next to me.

"Do you realize it has been three weeks since we returned from Golsara and I have never seen you in private?"

"I cannot come out of the home. I always think that Bardia might come home or telephone."

Saeed's laughter was quite nervous.

"And you don't want me to come to your place alone."

"Bardia doesn't like you. I think he is sensitive to any man that he thinks is close to me."

Now Saeed's answer was full of anger.

"He should realize that you are his mother, not his wife."

I felt helpless.

"Saeed, don't you hurt me, too. I can do nothing but be very careful with Bardia. As Soraya says, he needs my love and attention. I think he has changed a lot since I have put more time and effort in our relationship."

Saeed could not sit still anymore. Pretending that he was going to serve tea, he stood up and went to the kitchen. I could see that he was trying his best to control his anger. He had a very fragile temperament. The smallest thing could trigger his anger. But, at the same time, he wanted to be tolerant. So, whenever he was angry, he tried to escape an argument by shifting his attention to other subjects until he could control his anger. He usually fell quiet. It was as if he wanted to punish his opponent with such a sudden silence. He believed that his silence enabled him to control himself and stopped him from bothering others. But there was a heavy bitterness in his silence that was much more bothersome than any words or actions.

Nevertheless, I felt comfortable with Saeed. I did not feel that mysterious fright that Amin and Milan both sparked. I could tell him anything without fear of judgment. I enjoyed his presence without feeling that he wanted to impose his will on me. I felt that I had the right to think and act independently.

We spent a few hours together that afternoon but it was during that meeting that our insatiable desire for each other turned into an unreasonable anger. Our meeting ended with a bitter confrontation, the subject of which was the way I behaved toward Bardia. Although we apologized to each other the next day, our telephone conversation did not clear the air or reduce the tension. After that incident, I did not see Saeed in private for a very long time.

Now that I think about those days, I recognize that I could have seen him more often without Bardia knowing it. But I was too frightened to do anything of which Bardia disapproved, even in his absence.

• • • • •

It was during those one and a half months of living with Bardia that I could finally attend to the financial side of our lives as well. Hajji's lawyer had helped me transfer Amin's property to myself and the children. According to the Iranian law of inheritance, the widowed wife received only one eighth of the cash inheritance; thus, had Amin not purchased the building in my name, and had he not shared his bank account with me, I would not have owned anything after his death and would only have acted as a supervisor for my children's wealth until they reached the legal age. I would not have been able to sell or buy anything. Even this right of supervision was not sanctioned by the law — Hajji could always take it from me. I realized how safe I felt with all that wealth at my disposal. I saw the future of myself and the children as quite secure.

During those days, I also thought about selling the building and buying a big house in the north of Tehran, so that the children could be more comfortable. I had contacted a few real estate agents and had asked them to find suitable buyers for the building. I thought that it was the vastness of Hajji's house that made it more comfortable and attractive for the children and their friends. I would contemplate our new house. It had to have a floor plan similar to that of Hajji's with a separate part for Bardia. I mentally decorated the rooms with Hajji's place in mind.

I seldom thought about my job. The museum pieces, which I once loved so dearly, were fading away in my mind. Sometimes I asked myself why I didn't resign from the job. I certainly didn't need the money. I felt more comfortable at home. Most of the time, particularly when the children were at school and Fatemeh Khanum was cleaning the apartment, I stretched on the sofa and read a lighthearted book or ate chocolate and nuts.

In a short span of time, I began to feel that my dresses were becoming tight, sticking to my body. I had regained all of the weight I had lost after Amin's death. I had also gained an extra ten pounds. One night, when I was changing my clothes, I looked at myself in the mirror and saw the effect of that excess weight on my body. Saeed had praised it only some time ago with the words, "They cannot carve statues with such delicacy!" But I did not care. I only laughed and thought that if things continued as they were, I would soon end up with a body like Esmat Khanum. Nargess had mentioned my excessive weight a few times, but I had only shrugged in response.

"I have given up alcohol and medicine. This is quite natural. I feel fine."

I saw Nargess more than the others. She spent her mornings working for the planning section of the town council, and her afternoons in a remote house, attending to political meetings and preparing political literature and publications. Her evenings were spent at Ahmad's place. Before she went to Ahmad's, she always stopped by to see me briefly. I could detect the exhaustion in her face, but she was always happy and smiling. As soon as she arrived at my place, she took off her scarf, combed her hair with her long fingers, and sighed as if released from an intolerable burden. She was so unhappy about the scarf. "It is not the scarf itself," she would say. "It is the obligation behind it that kills me. I suffer because I am a woman and I have to be distinguished from others accordingly. It is not the scarf. It could be anything else, like a piece of ribbon on my head. I would feel the same way."

Ahmad was preparing his new paintings for an exhibition at the Faculty of Fine Arts. Nargess helped him with the frames, but Ahmad made the final decisions. Some evenings, when the children were in bed, or Bahram was asleep and Bardia was busy with his lessons in his room, I would go to Ahmad's apartment. Bardia came with me twice but he soon became bored and went back home.

I always admired Ahmad's paintings, especially his recent works inspired by the revolution. He talked to Nargess and me while he was working. In my opinion, his best painting was one he had entitled "Black Storm."

"To me, this is the clearest picture I can render about a revolution that has been hijacked by the Mullahs," he explained.

In the picture, a thick grove of black trees with interwoven branches and lofty trunks shaped like large boots plunged into the soil. Next to each boot, tiny white, yellow, and pink flowers scattered their green shoots. At the end of each shoot, a drop of blood oozed like a teardrop.

Ahmad excitedly explained how this picture had shaped in his mind. Once, he had seen a picture of members of a leftist guerrilla group standing in front of the firing squad. Then there was another picture that showed them strewn on the ground. Khalkhali, the infamously morbid Mullah known for his love of blood, stood in his black robe amongst his guards. Their shadows were cast on the dead bodies like black clouds.

I believed that this painting would attract attention and produce heated arguments, but it never reached the exhibition.

.15.

A few days had passed since Bardia had left for the camp. I missed him a lot; my staying at home waiting for his arrival became meaningless and dull. But, at the same time, I felt that a heavy burden had been lifted from my shoulders. I felt light and free. There was no one for whom I had to sit at home. I was not worried anymore about rushing to put on my scarf as soon as there was a knock at the door. Bardia wanted me to wear the scarf when he was with his friends, who usually accompanied him home every day.

The first time he asked me to wear it, I was furious. But I accepted his wishes without showing my anger. He was now my commander. The situation had recurred throughout my life. I had become a hostage of whomever was able to scare me. But, each time, I had only been able to recognize my situation when the man had completely overshadowed my life. This was not an easily attainable recognition. One can become addicted to her servitude, like a bird that does not dare fly away even when you open its cage after a long period of captivity. Or like someone who has lived in total darkness for a long time and, once you turn on the light, closes her eyes to take refuge in the darkness behind her eyelids.

Others could detect this addiction sooner and better. No one came to see me anymore, although I occasionally saw friends on Fridays at Hajji's place. As soon as Bardia left for the camp, however, everyone called on me. Saeed telephoned and said that he was coming to see me on Thursday. Soraya, whose relationship with her husband had recently dissolved, informed me that she was coming to see me on Thursday, as well. Nargess and Ahmad, who went to a movie every Thursday night, told me that they would join the others.

Although Bahram had caught a cold, forcing me to go to his room every now and then, that night turned out to be very pleasant. Soraya brought some homemade wine. After two months of sobriety, I became drunk with the first two glasses and flirted with Saeed in front of Soraya without feeling ashamed. Saeed got drunk and, as usual, sat there in silence, looking wondrously at others from behind his half-closed eyes with a smile. Whenever his eyes caught mine, they paused and I spied a fascinating twinkle in them that burned my soul and made my body shiver with ecstasy and desire.

Presumably, it was that eye contact that made Soraya leave the party sooner than expected. As soon as she left, Nargess and Ahmad went to Ahmad's apartment. After the golden times of Golsara, which seemed like a faraway dream, it was the first night that we had a few joyful hours to spend together.

Saeed began by blaming me about the way I was handling my life with Bardia, giving him all control and putting him in an authoritative position.

"This is against the interests of both you and your other child. It could well end up against the interests of Bardia as well," he said.

I begged him not to talk about those things. Although Bardia was not even in Tehran at the moment, I was afraid to let anyone enter his domain in his absence, even if the person was Saeed.

It was three in the morning when Saeed left my place. I did not want Bahram or Fatemeh Khanum see him there in the morning. Before he left, he made me promise to see him at least twice a week, when the children were at school. I accepted his suggestion without knowing that it was to be our last private meeting.

Once Saeed had gone, I went to look in on Bahram. In his sleep, he had a strange resemblance to Nargess that I had never noticed before. His cheeks, his slender nose, and his lips with their corners delicately drawn downwards were miniature replicas of Nargess's features. Esmat Khanum had repeatedly told us about how Bahram resembled a younger Nargess. I had looked for this resemblance and had not found it. But now I could see it there on his face. This was perhaps because Bahram had caught a cold that night and his nostrils were blocked. This had made him breathe with difficulty and created a mild shiver in his nose that resembled Nargess's nose when she got excited. I stood next to Bahram for a long time and thought that I should tell Nargess about my discovery in the morning.

A lot of noise coming from the corridor outside the apartment together with Nargess's muffled and incomprehensible voice woke me up. The clock next to the bed read twenty minutes past seven. I put on my bathrobe and went into the living room. The table was crowded with glasses and plates from the previous night. I went to

Bahram's room. He was fast asleep and breathed comfortably. I heard the noises from the corridor once again. I opened the front door and peeked out. Near the staircase, I could see a few Revolutionary Guards carrying a big parcel. In front of Ahmad's apartment, I saw Ahmad talking to two guards.

I closed the door, hastily put on my clothes, put the scarf on my head and went out of my apartment. Before I could reach Ahmad's place, a guard ran toward me, aimed his revolver at me, and shouted angrily.

"Get back inside your home, sister!"

I tried to say something, but I could not utter the words. The guard pushed me inside my apartment and closed the door with anger.

I stood motionless behind the door for a moment. Then I ran toward the kitchen and opened its door to the balcony. A white blanket of snow had fallen. There were a few cars and some more men in front of our building. The two guards were carrying Ahmad's painting, "The Black Storm," toward a van. I could see their footprints in the snow, forming the shape of a huge boot.

I went back inside the apartment and looked out of the peep hole on the front door. The hallway and the stairs seemed deserted but I did not dare open the door. I thought of calling Hajji but I remembered that he was not to know that Nargess had spent the night with Ahmad rather than me. I called Saeed instead. He answered with a sleepy voice.

"Saeed, the guards have invaded Ahmad's apartment. They're taking his paintings. I don't know what has happened to Nargess and Ahmad…. I don't…."

I was giving him this information half in Persian and half in English when I suddenly burst into tears. I cried out of fright.

"Easy, Luba, easy. Control yourself and tell me exactly what has happened. When did the guards come?" His voice was not sleepy anymore.

"I don't know…. But the whole building is full of them."

"Okay. Okay. You stay inside. Don't open the door to anyone. I'll be there soon."

I put the receiver down and went back to the balcony. I could not see the guards, and the cars were moving away. I tried to see the inside the cars, but it was impossible to do so from where I was standing. I returned to the hall, put my ear at the door, and tried to listen. There was no noise outside. I looked through the hole. There was no one there. Although Saeed had asked me not to open the door, I opened it slightly and looked out. The front door to Ahmad's apartment was closed and there was no one outside. I wanted to knock at the door, but I was not sure that the guards had left the apartment.

I closed the door and sat down next to my father. The light was slowly fading away and his face was becoming paler and fainter. There were two small, gaping holes on top of his left brow. I didn't dare move. I was afraid that the neighbors would see my shadow. I wanted them to think that I had left the place. I knew that the neighbors, despite their fears about helping us, would not say anything to the Agents. Everyone in that poverty stricken area hated them. Everyone but the spies. And I could not be sure if there was a spy amongst those eyes that had watched me secretly for the last few hours. I thought that the agents would soon return to take me away or that they would finish me with a silent bullet, leaving my body next to my father's. I was glad that Milan and I had separated a week ago and he would not return to our home. They would not find him here. Then I thought of Julia, the only one who would shelter me. But if they knew about my father, they would know about her as well. They had to know everything about Milan, me, and the other forty or so people who were connected to us. I longed for the night, which would give me a chance to escape. But the night was so far away and I sat there motionless and riddled with fear....

I heard the door being unlocked. I abruptly jumped up and stood in front of the door, ready to defend myself. It was only when Fatemeh Khanum entered the apartment that I realized that it was eight in the morning, the time she usually arrived on weekends. She was taken aback.

"What has happened? Anything wrong? Please, what is it?"

I crumpled down again and answered her in a soft voice, so soft that I thought she would not hear it.

"The guards were in Ahmad's place!"

"Our Ahmad Agha?"

She pointed to the next apartment. I nodded.

"And Nargess was there, too."

She sat next to me.

"Where is she now?"

"I don't know… I can't possibly know…."

My voice sounded helpless and frustrated. She stood up without saying anything else and went out the door. I heard her knocking at Ahmad's apartment. Some long moments later, she returned without any success.

"There is no one there. Have you told Hajji Agha about this?"

"No, but I've informed Saeed."

Calmly, she took my arms and led me to the living room, where I threw myself onto the cushions.

"I'll get you some tea," she said as she went into the kitchen.

She soon came back and began to clean up the table. She talked to me while putting the place in order.

"Some of them are just like this. They invade people's homes. They arrest people they don't know. But this time they have gone too far. You'll see how they'll back off as soon as they realize that they've arrested Hajji Agha's daughter. Don't you worry, Hajji Agha wouldn't let them say a harsh word to her. He wouldn't let them…."

She kept talking and I was scared that the guards would return and hear her from outside. But there was no energy left in me, not even enough energy to ask her either to lower her voice or to not to talk at all. My hands were shaking. I felt that I could only sit and weep helplessly. Just like Esmat Khanum. I tried to imagine what Nargess would do if she were in my place. I was sure that she would not remain silently at home if her apartment had been invaded by Revolutionary Guards. Why didn't I do anything? Why didn't I make any noise? Why didn't I tell them that she was Hajji Jalali's daughter? Why…? I hated myself. And Fatemeh Khanum was still talking.

The buzzer made me jump in my place but I was unable to ask Fatemeh Khanum not to open the door. With her usual quickness, she rushed to the hall, took the handset and asked who was downstairs. Then she pushed the button on the wall and looked at my inquiring eyes.

"It's Saeed Agha," she said.

Saeed, with his hair ruffled and his overcoat sprinkled with snow, sat down next to me. He took off the scarf, which was still on my head, and put it away.

"Don't worry, Luba. I told Abdol to talk to Hajji and take him to the Central Committee. They should be there now."

•   •   •   •   •

Saeed had not considered it wise to go with them. Although his face was not known and his articles were published under a pseudonym, a lot of his friends had joined various departments of the government after the revolution. They could recognize him. Therefore, he had to call Abdol, in spite of the fact that their friendship had been severed during the past few months. Abdol had no problem with the people in power and supported the government policies according to the directives laid down by the *Tudeh* Party.

Abdol had gone to Hajji's house and, without mentioning anything about Nargess, had asked him to come to the aid of Abdol's nephew, Ali, who was just a verbal supporter of Mojahedin. Abdol had told Hajji that Ali was arrested and his life was in danger. Hajji, while cursing the ignorant teenagers involved in the political turmoil, had gotten changed and left with Abdol.

"I didn't want to say this in front of Esmat Khanum. To be honest with you, they've arrested Ahmad and not Ali," Abdol told Hajji before he started the car.

"Who? Ahmad?"

"Yes."

"Why him? Is he a Communist?

"No, I don't know why they've arrested him. But... they've arrested Nargess, as well!"

Hajji turned his whole body toward Abdol with a sudden jump and stared at him with his mouth wide open. Abdol looked away and stammered that they both were arrested in Ahmad's place. Then he started the car and, before driving, he quickly added, "They are going to marry, you know."

He did not know why he lied. Perhaps he thought that such a lie would cover the ugliness of the fact that Nargess had been in Ahmad's place. Even before the Islamic Revolution, rarely would a woman stay in the house of a man who was not either her husband or a very close relative. The Revolution had added to the gravity of such matters. Everyday, the newspapers were full of reports on the executions or flogging of women who were involved in so-called "adultery."

Hajji's face had turned white and his eyes were full of tears. Abdol released the hand-brake and the car began to move.

"So why are you taking me there? Am I supposed to go ask them why they have arrested my daughter for adultery?" Hajji shouted with helpless anger.

Abdol continued driving for a while without saying a word. Then, in a low voice, he tried to convince Hajji.

"This is not adultery, my dear uncle. If a man and a woman are in a place together, that does not necessarily signify adultery. You know that. And they want to marry. They are considered engaged. You can say that you yourself have executed the religious ceremony."

"So you want me to tell lies. You want me to cover this shame with a lie. Is that so?"

"This is not a shameful thing, my dear uncle. You always say that marriage is nothing but the mutual consent of a man and a woman."

Abdol continued to persuade Hajji, who calmed down before they got to the Central Committee building. As Abdol followed Hajji up the stairs, he could not help but admire the old man, who faced a difficult situation so gracefully. To Abdol, it seemed so painful that such a man should have to hide his wounded pride from the inquisitive eyes of the committee members.

When they entered the building, they noticed an obvious abundance of activity. Telephones rang and the head of the committee, a high-ranking Mullah, went back and forth between rooms. He finally informed them that Ahmad would be released in twenty-four hours but Nargess could be taken home from the Amirieh Committee the same day.

But, just before Hajji stood up from his chair, the head of the Central Committee had some other words to say.

"I hope you'll excuse all of us, sir. I'm so ashamed. Damn these innocent but ignorant youngsters…. They've… They've flogged your estimable daughter before any proper investigation…."

Hajji was totally shocked. He pounded his fist on his knee and nearly shouted out.

"Allah is the greatest. Allah is the greatest."

He repeated this verse from the Holy Koran, which Muslims utter in moments of distress, extreme danger, or even joy. Hajji turned his face away from the official. The man looked at Abdol, who was trying his best to control himself. The man spoke again in a low voice.

"I wish they had their papers with them. Something to show that they were religiously recognized as husband and wife."

"How can people know when you're going to invade? How?"

Hajji nearly shouted. Then he stood up. The Mullah, pretending to be ashamed of what had happened, escorted them to the door. He did not dare hand the release order to Hajji. He gave the letter to Abdol. Hajji neither looked at him nor said farewell. He began descending the stairs. On the first step, his knees buckled. Abdol hurried toward him and took his arms, leading him toward the street.

From the street, Hajji looked at the building. It was the old House of Parliament, the remainder of the liberal Constitutional Revolution of some sixty years ago. Now it housed the Central Islamic Revolutionary Committee.

"You had better take Nargess to your home. Esmat Khanum shouldn't see her for a while. And call me a taxi," Hajji said.

•　•　•　•　•

Saeed's insistence that I not go to Soraya's house did not change my mind. I put the scarf on my head and went there with him. There was a period of four hours between the time they had taken Ahmad and Nargess away and when Abdol called to tell us that Nargess was with him and Ahmad would be released the next day. I had regained my control during this period, but I saw that Saeed had become more and more impatient as time passed. He had phoned several people and had asked them to cancel all of their appointments. He seemed to guess that one of the occasional waves of arrests had begun once again. He had restlessly walked back and forth in the room between calls as if trying to put the clues together to find out why Ahmad and Nargess had been arrested. When Abdol called to give us the news of Nargess's release, Saeed grabbed the phone from me.

"Tell me what has happened."

He listened for a while. His face turned red.

"I'll come there right away," he said at last.

"I'm going to come and see her too," I said.

He tried to convince me not to go with him. But, seeing that I would not change my mind, he told me about Nargess's ordeal.

"You won't be able to take it, Luba," he said.

His words revealed how feeble I had become in others' eyes. I was so angry with myself for the weakness I had shown that morning. Instead of answering him, I told Fatemeh Khanum to prepare Bahram so that we could drop him off at Hajji's house before going to Abdol's.

Soraya's eyes were red with tears when she opened the door.

"She is sleeping. I have given her strong tranquilizers."

"I want to see her," I said.

Soraya wordlessly led me to the bedroom. Nargess was lying on the bed face-down. Her body was covered with a white sheet; and I could only see her naked shoulders and her long braided hair. I moved around the bed to be able to see her face. It was pale and swollen like the face of someone who had fallen asleep after a long cry.

"Her wounds are deep. Those bastards treated her awfully," Soraya murmured.

I took a corner of the sheet and lifted it slowly. Soraya took the other corner.

"Be careful," she said.

She held up the sheet. Nargess was completely naked. Her usually pinkish skin now resembled the gray, baked clay statuettes of the goddess Anahita when just brought out of the earth. There was a cross-hatching of red oblique lines on her buttocks and the back of her thighs. The flesh had burst her skin open and seemed pale under a thick layer of creamy ointment. Here and there, a small brook of blood disturbed the geometrical order of the lines, which mingled together near her knees, plowing her young skin.

I let the sheet go and Soraya stretched it carefully on Nargess.

I had to lean on a wall. Stella took off her thick stockings angrily and showed her feet to Milan. "Don't tell me to carry on…. I cannot take it anymore. I cannot bear it. Tell me I'm a coward. Tell me I'm weak. Yes, I am weak. But how can you know if you, too, are a coward if you have not been in my situation?" Her raised foot trembled in front of Milan. It was covered with dark blue lines. A year had passed since her release and she had not told us anything about her ordeal.

Milan held her ankle and slowly put it back down on the floor. "But they didn't know what you were doing at that time. Why did they do this to you?"

Stella saw my wet eyes and looked down. Then she put her stockings back on. "I don't know. Perhaps they had discovered a certain potential in me and were thwarting it. As you see, they've been successful."

"Let's go to the other room," Soraya murmured.

Saeed and Abdol were in the living room, talking softly. I thought to myself that, again, another family matter had brought them together. They stopped talking once we entered the room.

"When is she supposed to return to consciousness?" Saeed asked.

"Not for at least another three hours," Soraya answered.

Saeed stood up. "I'd better go and see what can be done for Ahmad," he said.

"Isn't he going to be released tomorrow?" I asked.

Abdol answered my question.

"They said that to Hajji. But when I went to the committee, it seemed to me that Ahmad was in real trouble."

"Nargess was also worried about Ahmad," Soraya added. "She said that they didn't expect her to be at his place. It means that they had not intended to arrest two adulterers. It seems that they were mostly concerned with his paintings. Nargess was not in a condition to give us any more information."

"I'll be back in a few hours," Saeed said. He left the room.

●   ●   ●   ●   ●

Ahmad and Nargess were asleep in the same bed when the knocking came at the door. It was so soft that only Ahmad noticed it and, perhaps thinking that it was me, he got dressed and opened the door. Immediately, five guards rushed into the apartment. One of them hit Ahmad's chest with the stock of his machine gun until Ahmad fell down. Ahmad's deep moans woke Nargess up. Still in her night gown, she hurried to the hall and saw guards and Ahmad, stretched out on the ground. Shocked, she ran back into the bedroom and put the bed sheet around her shoulders. Then, hoping to wake me and Saeed, whom she believed to be still in my apartment, she began to shout.

"Who are you? Why are you here?"

The guards, who had not expected someone else to be in the apartment, were surprised and ran after her. One of them waved his revolver in front of her face and shouted at her.

"Shut up, you bloody whore. Do you think we have sacrificed so many martyrs so that you can enjoy your life like this?"

Another guard came forward, took her hand, and pushed her onto the sofa.

"Why have you come here?" Nargess shouted again.

This was the muffled sound that I had heard.

The guards quickly tied her hands and feet, put the bed sheet on her head and pushed her toward the front door. Before her head was completely covered by the sheet, Nargess saw that a guard had wrapped Ahmad in something resembling clothing and was pushing him out of the door. Ahmad was bent over and could only walk with difficulty.

Once at the committee building, officials asked Nargess questions about her relationship with Ahmad without asking her identity.

"We are engaged. We are going to marry shortly."

Nargess hoped that Ahmad would say the same thing.

But the investigators didn't believe her.

"Engaged! The hell with you. You bastard adulterers!"

"But you can ask my father. You surely know him. He is...."

The investigator did not let her finish.

"Shut up! Don't say anything unless you're asked."

He was shouting furiously. Then he murmured to himself.

"There is not a grain of truth in whatever these bastards say."

Soon he began to ask about Ahmad's paintings, which were brought in, wet, broken and dirty, to be shown to her. They wanted her to tell them about the meaning of all the scenes.

Her answers were short. "There is no special meaning to that... It's just a kind of play with colors." Throughout the ordeal, she hoped that I had heard her voice and had informed Hajji. She expected her father to be there any moment.

Finally, "The Black Storm" was brought in. Some of the little flowers were covered with water and mud.

"You should know this one very well. Don't you? The cloak of his excellency Khalkhali and the execution of anti-revolutionary elements...."

"I don't understand paintings. I cannot find any special meaning in this," she said hastily.

"You anti-revolutionary adulterer! So, now, you don't understand it!"

He ordered the others to take Nargess away. Nargess was glad, thinking that the postponement of her interrogation was in her favor.

The guards came towards her, stuffed her mouth with a towel, and took her out. She struggled under the sheet, which was again wrapped around her head. They took her into the open yard and laid her down on a wet, wooden bench. Then two women, their faces covered with black veils, held her ankles with firm hands. Two other women sat on her hands. A guard had a metal flog in his hand. He whirled the flog above his head and hit Nargess's back with all his might.

Nargess could remember only up to the fifteenth stroke. She could not continue counting the strokes, which were supposed to reach eighty. At the beginning, the shooting pain made her hit her head on the wooden bench. But soon, one of the women held her head firmly to prevent her from doing so. It was at that moment that Nargess saw Ahmad being forced to lay on another bench. Then, despite the woman's attempts, her head dropped down.

She regained consciousness when she felt the women pour cold water on her face. She felt no pain but was very cold. This coldness made her body shake uncontrollably. The towel was not in her mouth. Her hands and feet were not tied up. But her jaws were locked and she felt her hands and feet trembling to an unknown rhythm. It was as if they were trying to escape from the rest of her body.

One of the women was sitting next to her on the ground, murmuring some words that did not resemble the other woman's constant curses. Nargess could not remember what she said for a long time. It was only three months later that she recalled them.

"Her voice was deep and muffled, as if she was crying. She said, 'Seek repentance. What you are suffering is nothing in comparison to what you'll get in the other world.'"

The women carried Nargess to one of the committee rooms. They laid her face-down on the carpet and left her, except for the woman who had been crying. She braided Nargess's hair, covered her body with a sheet, and left the room after telling Nargess that she would bring her a cup of hot tea.

But soon, two Revolutionary Guards entered the room and sat on the chairs next to her. Nargess could see their new wet boots. One of them began to speak in a careful, polite voice. "Are you Miss Nargess Jalali?"

Nargess could not unlock her jaws to answer him. She only thought, "My father must be here." And the pain returned with an unexpected power so shattering that the tremble in her hands and feet stopped.

● ● ● ● ●

Before Nargess could regain consciousness, Abdol decided to see how Hajji was coping with the incident and left Soraya and me alone. It was a chance for Soraya to tell me about the chaotic situation of her own married life.

Nargess's voice made us hurry toward the bedroom. She turned her head in the direction of the door and, as soon as she saw me, there was a glitter in her swollen eyes and a smile on her lips.

"Thank God that your sleep was not that deep!" she said.

I sat next to her on the bed and kissed her cheek. She tried to shift her body to lie on her side, but she could not do so. She moaned. When she hunched her shoulders from the pain, the chasm between her shoulder blades swallowed her long neck. I held her cold hand.

"It seems that you have to stay in this position for a while," I said.

A tiny smile shone on her pained face.

"Any news of Ahmad?" Nargess asked.

Soraya moved her chair forward.

"Saeed has gone to see what can be done for him."

Nargess was looking at her frightfully. Then she turned away and gazed at a corner of the room. A few seconds later, while biting her lower lip so hard that I expected blood to ooze out of it, she began to murmur again.

"It's so hard to imagine those animals keeping him in jail for another night."

It was as if Nargess herself was standing safely on the shore, worrying about someone caught in the danger of the rough sea. She did not know that, only three and a half years later, she would return to those animals and stay in their cage not for a night, not for a month, and not even just for a year. Three and a half years later, two young girls and a teenaged boy, all considered supporters of Mojahedin, happened to meet Nargess while escaping from the guards. They asked her for help. Nargess hid them in Golsara for forty-five days and later took them to Kurdistan to help them cross the border to seek refuge in Turkey. In Kurdistan, she was arrested by the guards. Although there was a gap of three and a half years between the day I sat next to her flogged body and the day she was arrested in Kurdistan, whenever I return to my memories of Iran, these two pictures meld together; the present and the future, which now are both part of the past, then become one.

"They'll release him tomorrow, for sure," Soraya said.

Nargess released her lower lip and the fear faded from her eyes.

"Where is Abdol?" she asked.

"He went to see Hajji."

Upon hearing her father's name, Nargess became gloomy and moaned as if she was once more attacked by the pain.

"Poor Mom and Dad…. Their daughter has been flogged for adultery!"

Soraya told her that Esmat Khanum was not aware of what had happened and believed that everyone was at Homeira's house for the day. Nargess was relieved. After a short pause, she changed the subject.

"I don't know…. I don't understand how they found out about the paintings…."

She was interrupted by Saeed's knocking at the door. Soraya left the room to let him in. Nargess kept talking.

"No one but you and I had ever seen the paintings. But the committee knew so much about them."

Although she was not implying anything, I was annoyed. It was as if she had accused me of spying.

"I don't get what you're trying to say. No one but you and me…."

Saeed interrupted me. He was standing next to me, smiling at Nargess. "I see. I see. You're even better than me!" he said.

Then he kissed her cheek and sat down. Nargess continued.

"Why did you get so defensive? You are becoming very sensitive. Why did you think I was implying something about you?"

Then she explained to Saeed what had been going on between us.

"I think someone knew about the paintings and informed the guards."

"But no one had seen them besides you and me," I said.

Nargess pursed her lips and murmured, "We don't know."

We sat next to her bed until late that evening. Saeed and Nargess reviewed in full detail what she had heard and said to the committee. They concluded that there might have been a microphone planted in Ahmad's room.

"But how on earth could they do that?" I asked, frightened.

"Easy. When no one is at home, they come in like thieves and plant it. All of us could have such devices planted in our homes," Saeed explained.

"Might there be one in my home, too?"

The idea was so frightful that I felt a sudden shiver in my body and remembered the last night at my place.

"It's not improbable. We have to search all of our houses," Nargess answered. She looked at Saeed and continued. "It would be better if you took Shahram to Luba's home tomorrow to search thoroughly."

.16.

I did not dare go back home that night. I stayed at Soraya's overnight and returned home early in the morning, before Fatemeh Khanum arrived. Once she came, I asked her to go to Hajji's place and look after Bahram.

It was around ten when Saeed and Shahram arrived. Shahram was a prominent member of Fada'iyan, an independent communist guerrilla group in Iran. He was condemned to death in absentia during the Shah's regime and had returned to Iran after the revolution. While outside of Iran, he studied computer science and trained as a guerrilla for two years in Eastern Europe and China. One of his fields of expertise was discovering hidden microphones and cameras, as well as time bombs. He and Saeed were friends when I met Saeed in England. I had seen him a few times there and once in Iran, at Saeed's place, after the revolution.

It was during that last meeting when Shahram ridiculed Amin's opinions about the revolution. Despite his usual indifference, Amin was caught off guard and became very upset. We had to leave the party sooner than expected.

Shahram was short, skinny, and usually cheerful. But, that day, when he entered the apartment, he seemed tired, anxious, and thinner than ever. Saeed had told me that no one should talk while they were searching for microphones. We only shook hands. Shahram smiled at me, put his large briefcase down and took a small device out of his pocket.

He began in the living room. He passed the device over items with quick, precise movements: around the picture frames, all over the sofas and chairs, under the tables, around the lampshades. He searched the kitchen with the same attentiveness. Then Saeed led him to the library. His search there lasted longer than his searches of the living room and the kitchen. He examined all of the bookshelves. When Saeed noticed that Shahram could not reach the upper shelves, he went to the kitchen and brought back a short metal ladder. He climbed the ladder and searched those shelves as well.

I had nothing to do but sit at the dinner table and anxiously smoke a cigarette. This anxiety took me back in time. We were young and fresh-faced. Whenever we had a clandestine meeting, we would turn on two radio sets as loud as possible tuned to two different stations. Then we sat close to the walls and talked in very soft voices. Whenever we spoke too loudly, Milan pointed his finger at us and reminded us to lower our voices. Still, I was always frightened by the thought that there might have been a microphone planted in that place.

When I led Shahram to my bedroom, I was shaking silently with the fear that there could be a microphone in there. Saeed, who saw me shivering, put his hand on my shoulder and pressed my body against his. Shahram searched under the bed, around the mirror, inside the drawers, under the picture frames and even under the vases. There was nothing there.

Then we went into Bardia's room. Shahram searched under Bardia's bed and inside his closet. Next, he tried to open the first drawer in Bardia's desk. It was locked. While sitting there, he beckoned to me with his finger and murmured in my ear, "Where is the key?" I shrugged. I actually did not even know that Bardia locked his drawers. Shahram went out of the room and returned with a bunch of keys. The drawers were unlocked in a matter of minutes. In the first drawer, Shahram took out a box from under a pile of papers, and looked at it. He opened the next drawer. There was something like a medium-sized radio inside. He took it out, put it on the desk, and, like someone who had just run a long distance, took a deep breath. He showed the box to us.

"These are the microphones that once belonged to SAVAK. Now the new people use it."

Then he pointed to the device on the desk.

"And this is the receiver that works with the microphones. It has a range of ten miles."

I moved toward him in bewilderment. In the box, there were about twenty little microphones, each as big as a button.

"Do you mean that they've planted microphones here, as well?" I asked in a low voice.

Saeed looked away and Shahram answered my question bluntly.

"No. There is no microphone planted in this apartment."

"So what are these?" I asked, not believing my eyes.

"These microphones would not be of any use without this receiver." Saeed started to explain but he did not finish his sentence. On the day before, he and Nargess had come to the conclusion that Bardia was the one who had planted the microphone in Ahmad's apartment. They had not yet informed me of their conclusion. I sat on the edge of Bardia's bed and spoke slowly.

"Do you mean to say that Bardia has done this?"

Shahram stood up. He put the box and the receiver back in the drawers and rearranged the items as they were before.

"Your son shouldn't know that you're aware of this. This knowledge could endanger others, as well as yourself," he said.

I looked at Shahram with fright and shame. An old familiar picture was resurfacing in my mind. Without speaking, Stursa had taken my father to the garden for a talk. One of my father's feet was on the edge of the flowerbed. He was leaning on the magnolia tree — exactly where I found his body some years later. I was holding him in my arms.

"You have to be very careful," Stursa said. "Jerome is with them. I know that he spies on others for them. Hasn't he been around here recently?"

"No. Since I took Marta to the hospital, I haven't seen him." "Good. Then they are not suspicious about you. Nevertheless, you should be very careful. Tell the others to be on guard as well. They should watch him carefully."

From that day on, whenever I saw Julia, Jerome's daughter, I had mixed feelings. I was afraid, but at the same time, I felt pity for her. She was a happy, boisterous girl, but the other children were reluctant to let her inside their circles. The boys called her "a piece of yellow shit," and the girls referring to her yellowish hair and round face called her "yellow pumpkin." She did not pay any attention. She noisily interfered with other children's games and, amid laughter and jokes, made them let her play. I liked her self-confidence and admired the way she did not pay any attention to what others thought and said. But from that day on, I was too afraid of her to venture close to her. Was she also a spy, like her father?

"Do you think Bardia is a spy?" I asked Saeed.

Saeed looked away, toward the window.

"He may not know what he is doing. But what he does could indeed be called spying."

There was a big lump in my throat. I could hardly resist the tears pouring out of my eyes.

"He's only fourteen.... Do you understand? Fourteen. In what other part of the world would they make a fourteen-year-old child spy on others?"

Shahram closed his briefcase.

"Here they are capable of doing anything. Just as Hitler did."

Saeed and Shahram left the apartment and I returned to Bardia's room. I sat on his bed, in front of his desk. The room had not changed since he left for the camp. It was in that room that I had held him in my arms and had told him, "Promise me that you'll take good care of yourself."

Excited by his upcoming trip, he had taken his suitcase and moved toward the door.

"Okay. I promise."

He had left the apartment before I could reach him. Nargess, who was standing in the hall, was amazed.

"He even didn't say goodbye to me."

"That's because he was so happy. He couldn't pay any attention to anything but his trip."

"I'm so worried about him. These training camps do not have a good effect on children. I wish you'd prevented him from going on this trip."

I did not respond to her, but I thought about the time when I was Bardia's age. Didn't I go to camps? Didn't I stand for hours to listen to the men and women who praised Stalin and the leaders of the Communist Party? Hadn't I stood in the town's squares to applaud them? Hadn't I swayed those red flags so hard that when I got home at night, my muscles were swollen and painful with fatigue?

"When are they going to leave these children alone?" my mother would say. I could not understand my mother's objections. I only knew that I loved those activities, especially the spinning of the red flags. As they moved faster and faster, the rainbow they made, and the words written in that rainbow, seemed even more magnificent.

"You may not be familiar with this kind of experience, but all of my childhood was spent in such demonstrations, gatherings, speeches, and training camps. But what did I gain from them other than my hatred for all of it?" I told Nargess.

"Did all of those children share your hatred later on? Don't you think that if others felt like you, you would be in your own country now?" she answered back with a smile.

My response was quick and involuntary. "Bardia won't keep this attitude. Give him some time and he'll change completely."

Now, a few days after that conversation, I was sitting in Bardia's room. Besides Nargess and Ahmad, I wondered how many others Bardia had betrayed into imprisonment and torture. I wondered who else was next to face such an ordeal. I did not know what to do with him.

Before leaving my home, Shahram had told me, "Take him out of Iran with you. That is the only solution for him."

But I did not have the power to force Bardia to come with me. In the past one and a half months, I had noticed that he did not pay any attention to anything that I told him. He did everything as he wished. In fact, it was I who had become submissive toward him. I had done whatever he had told me to do. I could not see how I was to resist his wishes in the future.

"I don't have any influence on him. Even when I made him return home, I had to ask for the help of his schoolmaster. His grandfather even helped me to do it. How could I ask the schoolmaster to advise him to leave the country with me?" I asked Shahram.

Saeed, evidently uneasy, shook his head and addressed Shahram.

"He is involved with those people much more than you think. They wouldn't let him go that easily. They need children like Bardia."

Then he looked at me.

"I am worried about you and Bahram. I think it would be better if you two went abroad, at least for a few months. There might be some changes by then."

I looked at him with reproach.

"You want me to go without Bardia? Just when he needs me most? I have to be here to save him. That is what I need to do."

Left alone in Bardia's room, I thought about possible ways to save him from the religious fundamentalists who called themselves members of the *Hezbollah* (Party of God). I could find none. They were holding the law in their hands, the very law that denied me all of the rights a mother should have over her children. Every fourteen-year-old boy was considered to be lawfully independent. He could easily leave his parental home, cast votes in elections, carry weapons, marry, or become a spy. No, I could not save him. But I had to stay with him. I could not leave him alone in a society which was increasingly becoming crazier and crazier. I did not want to accept that my Bardia did not exist but within my own illusions.

The large picture of Bardia that hung over his desk was taken when he was five years old. He was standing next to Amin, near the lions' cage. I had taken the picture at the London Zoo. He had put his hand on his waist and was looking proudly at the lions. Next to it, there was another picture taken on his eleventh birthday. He was looking at the camera, at me, and his eyes were filled with a childish happiness.

● ● ● ● ●

Ahmad remained in jail. Hajji, and those of his friends who had attained high offices in the government after the presidency of Bani-Sadr, tried their best to get him out, but to no avail. Although the new public prosecutor, whom everyone knew as "The Revolutionary Butcher," belonged to a group of clergy that did not openly want to antagonize Hajji, he behaved quite differently. Every week, Ahmad's release was postponed to the next, each time with a new excuse.

Nargess returned home after two weeks. Everyone, including Esmat Khanum, believed that she had spent that time at Golsara. After her return, she was allowed to see Ahmad once. Hajji personally had obtained permission for this meeting from the public prosecutor. She visited Ahmad in the presence of Revolutionary Guards. Although Ahmad had seemed ill, he had told her that he was fine. Other than that, he only gave "yes" or "no" answers to Nargess's questions. Nargess had given cigarette packs and other things she had brought for him to the guards. She had returned home in a miserable mood.

Bardia returned home as well, with a tanned face and a large paramilitary coat. While he was replacing his childhood pictures on the wall of his room with new ones, I asked him, "Did you know that poor Ahmad is in jail?"

He did not look at me.

"You could see that he was anti-revolutionary. He was a Bahá'í as well."

The young man in the picture, wearing a paramilitary coat and carrying a machine gun, had no resemblance to my Bardia. I tried to sound indifferent.

"But if he was Bahá'í, why didn't he go to America along with his family?"

Bardia turned back and, still standing on the chair, began to talk like a father to a young daughter.

"Those who have not left the country are here to cause trouble. You don't know these things. They are all agents of America."

It was the first time he had spoken to me in that manner.

"I dearly wish that they release him soon. You know, he is going to marry your Auntie Nargess."

Bardia jumped down and came toward me, waving the hammer in his hand in a threatening way.

"Auntie Nargess? When?"

His eyes were not Bardia's eyes anymore. A gray and ruthless dust covered them. I looked away and sat down.

"Your grandpa has already performed the religious ceremony himself."

"When did this happen?"

"Sometime before they arrested him. Didn't you notice that Nargess spent most of her nights in his apartment?"

Bardia climbed onto the chair again to drive another nail into the wall.

"I have to talk to Grandpa," he said.

I looked at the new picture on the wall. In it, Khomeini stood behind Bardia, who kneeled in front of him. Khomeini's hand was on Bardia's head. It reminded me of an ancient bas-relief on southern Iranian mountains showing the Roman Emperor, Valerian, kneeling in front of Shahpour, the Iranian king.

I walked toward the door. The two childhood pictures lay near the door. I took them and walked out in silence.

What I told Bardia was what Hajji, Nargess, and I had previously agreed to say. Hajji, too, was aware that Bardia had spied on Ahmad. We had agreed that no one else should know about this shame. But was this secret to remain as untold as the other secrets about Bardia's life? Or was there to be someone amongst our group — Abdol, Soraya, Nargess, Hajji, Saeed, or Shahram — who would disclose it? I had come to the conclusion that in Iran, only rarely did a secret remain undisclosed. Everyone talked to each other in a secretive way and ended the gossip by saying, "Please keep this to yourself." But I had never heard of a secret remain silent. Therefore, I had to expect, after a while, that wherever I went, people would begin to talk to me with some trepidation. After all, I was the mother of a spy. I could tell him a secret unintentionally.

The Julia of ten years later, young and attractive, combatant and untiring, had touched her short, wheat-colored hair and laughed. "Even I was afraid of myself. I dared not look at other children's eyes. I did not listen to any of them, so that I would not hear something that I was not supposed to know. I never asked any questions. I used to think that I was the loneliest girl in the world."

And I knew that my total loneliness and separation had begun with Bardia's return from the training camp.

.17.

That one-month training course had more effect on Bardia than anything else he had learned in his fourteen years. He had turned into an irritable, aggressive, and stern young man. He considered himself a guardian of Islam and the revolution and honored this title as an inheritance bestowed to him by his "martyred" father. In the evenings, he hurried home, hastily put his briefcase and books in his room, donned his paramilitary coat, and, without explaining anything to me, said, "I'm leaving," and disappear. He never returned home before ten o'clock at night. Sometimes he returned at eleven. Once, I asked him about it.

"Where do you go at night?"

"To the mosque."

The mosques were turned into offices for Revolutionary Committees in each locality. It was in these committees that decisions were made on confiscating properties, arresting anti-revolutionaries, spying on people, and controlling behaviors and attitudes. These buildings were used as temporary jails for those who were to stay overnight. They arrested people at night in their homes or in the streets and took them to the mosques. There, after a short interrogation, they were sent to the huge prisons around the city. These prisons, built by the Shah's regime, had been emptied during the revolution by people who had opened them. After the revolution they were, again, full of new prisoners.

The newly elected president had no real power. He was a name and a mouth, that daily promised a better, more comfortable, and more secure life for Iranians. None of his promises had the tiniest chance of staying valid even until his speeches were finished. There were local uprisings all over the country. Leftists were massacred by the hundreds. The state apparently was not involved in these massacres. They were the works of the state-backed guards and vagabonds who plundered the country without fear of the government's reaction. They knew that not only would there be no punishment for their actions, but also that their services were appreciated by the leaders of the revolution.

The *Hezbollah*, which had never been formally announced as a political party and had no headquarters, recruited mobsters and youngsters in secretive haste. Whoever carried a weapon and announced his allegiance to the "Line of the Imam" was a member of *Hezbollah*, felt free to do whatever he wished. They arrested whomever they wanted, invaded any home they deemed necessary, and labeled anyone they wished as agents of America and Israel. At night, all of the people in the streets were exposed to their control. Although it had not been declared, a state of siege was in force. In the streets, they stopped women who were not dressed according to Islamic regulations and took them to the committees. If the women were accompanied by men, they were asked to produce documents verifying their relationship. If a woman could not prove that the man was either her husband or a member of her immediate family, she was arrested, jailed, and flogged. At night, *Hezbollah* members stopped cars, told the passengers to come out, and smelled their breath. If they could detect the smell of alcohol, the passengers were flogged. A well-known poet had written a short poem that everybody repeated: "They sniff your breath/ to see if you have said/ I love you." Gradually, all the signs of joy, love, and peacefulness were being forbidden.

The Iranian New Year started on the first day of spring. But that year, the streets were empty. There was none of the usual excitement and fireworks that signaled the happiness of the holiday. The festivities were reminiscent of those in pre-Islamic Iranian history; therefore, the new regime considered them pagan ceremonies. Those who wanted to observe the traditional ceremonies did not dare do so in the open. Nevertheless, most people were determined to do what they wanted at home, although on a small scale and in a discreet manner. They were usually better off at home. Restaurants and public places were mostly deserted. As soon as offices and shops closed, everyone rushed home to the freedom within the four walls of their small abodes, where guards and *Hezbollah* members usually could not check their every movement.

Because I had a member of *Hezbollah* at home, I had not yet understood the depth of the fear the name instilled in others. I had not yet associated members of *Hezbollah* with those secret service agents who had filled my youth with horrific nightmares. The Revolutionary Guard represented no one but my son, my little Bardia, who suddenly had revolted against the whole world. To me, his revolt was a consequence of adolescence. But it was exactly what others shunned. Rarely did anyone call on me. Nargess telephoned me every now and then. Saeed did the same, but on a much more limited basis. They just wanted to know how I was. Their words were limited and short. I knew they believed that the line could be tapped. But Esmat Khanum, perhaps blissfully ignorant of what had happened in the country and the family, kept calling me every day. Unlike in the past, I now liked her chats and even encouraged them with my casual questions.

I considered my loneliness unimportant. Even the excitement that used to inflame my body with the desire to hold Saeed in my arms was gradually fading away. Instead, it was replaced by a kind of abstinent resignation. I tried my best not to confront him at all. All of my emotions concentrated on Bardia. I believed that he was a lonely person and that I shared this loneliness with him. I believed he needed my extreme love to compensate for his aloofness. I had even forgotten Bahram. He was usually busy with his homework. He played in the solitude of his room. He was happiest when his brother arrived home.

Had that incident in mid-spring not occurred, I do not know how far I might have followed Bardia.

● ● ● ● ●

Bardia usually never came home later than eleven o'clock. But one night, midnight arrived and he did not show up. I paced between the living room and the kitchen more than a hundred times; each time, I watched the street from the balcony and searched for the committee jeep that usually brought him home every night. I knew the sound of its brakes in front of the building. As soon as I heard that sound, I would usually run into the kitchen, put Bardia's food on the stove, and wait for him to open the front door.

When midnight passed, I could not tolerate waiting for him anymore. I put a scarf on my head and drove to a mosque near Alborz Street, where I knew he usually worked. Once, when we passed the mosque, Bardia had pointed and proudly announced, "This is our committee!"

While I was parking the car near the mosque, I noticed a few armed young men standing in front of the building. I walked cautiously toward them but, before I could reach them, one of them approached me. While putting his hand on his machine gun, he shouted at me.

"What do you want, sister?"

"I've come for my son," I said reluctantly.

The young man, about sixteen years old, sounded stern.

"Who is your son?"

Other young men, their grim faces distorted by the light coming from the mosque, also came forward and encircled me. Evidently they thought that my son had been arrested and was being kept at the committee. I was horrified.

"I've come for Bardia. Bardia Jalali."

The first boy dropped his hands at his sides and the others moved away. The boy's voice sounded childish now.

"Forgive me, mother. I did not recognize you. I'll call him right away."

He ran inside the mosque and came back a few moments later with Bardia. I had kept my eyes down so as not to look at the boys in front of the mosque, but I looked up upon hearing their footsteps. With his head raised and a machine gun on his shoulder, Bardia came toward me. Without saying a word, he gently took my arm and led me toward the road and away from the other boys. When we got to the car, he began to talk in a voice which sounded coarser than ever.

"Why have you come here?" he asked.

I released my arm from his grip and opened the car door.

"I was so worried about you. Do you know what time it is?"

He did not say anything. He waited until I was inside the car and closed the door.

"I'll be home in one hour."

The ride between the mosque and our building was not more than five minutes but it seemed like a few hours to me. All I could do was replay images of the young men in front of the mosque, Bardia with a machine gun, Bardia going back to the others while I drove away.

It had seemed to me that the shoulder that carried the gun had dropped and the other shoulder moved awkwardly. He was like someone whose feet were not the same length. Four years later, when I was informed that Bardia had returned from the war with a bullet hole in his leg and would be lame for the rest of his life, the image of his uneven shoulders came back to mind.

I do not remember when Bardia returned that night. I sat crossed-legged on the sofa and smoked cigarette after cigarette, which I now did much more often than I used to. I asked myself if Bardia could ever become an ordinary boy again. In London, during Bardia's childhood, whenever I saw a young drug addict on a bench in the street or in a park, I would think about Bardia's future with anxiety. Once I asked Amin, "Why don't the parents of these young people do anything to save them?"

"They cannot be saved anymore. They're already dead, but their names have not yet been removed from the list of those who are alive," he said. But I could not believe that there was nothing left to do for them.

Now, I kept asking myself, "What can I do for Bardia?"

When Bardia finally came home, I realized that I could do nothing for him. He was dead and I was supposed to carry his corpse on my shoulders until the end of time.

He was stern and aggressive. Before I could say anything, he spoke with a harsh voice.

"Do you think that I'm still a little child whom you still need to look after?"

As usual, I tried to be non-confrontational.

"If it had been your father who was late, I would have tried to find him, as well. Why don't you consider my feelings?"

"Do not come after me ever again. I will be as late as I want. You are not to come after me."

I tried to speak forcefully.

"What kind of a place is that? A mosque or an army barrack? You are not old enough to carry a machine gun."

He laughed as if on the verge of going mad.

"I am old enough to know what I'm doing," he said.

I tried to remain calm.

"Believe me, Bardia. There is no other place in the world where a child your age would be allowed to carry a gun."

"Here, it is different from the rest of the world. This is a Muslim and revolutionary country. I'm free to do whatever I like. Whatever. Do you understand?"

His face had no resemblance to that of my Bardia. There was something in it that I had never seen or known before. Even now, ten years after that night, whenever I remember that face, I become frightened. I remember that I looked down and held my knees in my arms. My voice came out of my throat with tremendous difficulty.

"What has happened to you, Bardia? I am your mother."

He turned away. The carpet shrunk under the pressure of his boots, which reflected the red of the flowers on the rug.

"Islam and the revolution are more important than anything else to me."

I do not know why I next said what I did.

"I have remained in this country for the sake of my children. If this is not important to you, I'll go away."

He turned to me once again and put his hand on my shoulder. The weight of his hand amazed me. I looked up to make sure it was Bardia who touched my shoulder. His eyes, which no longer resembled mine, were cold and cruel. He shouted at me.

"You can go wherever you like. Neither Bahram nor I need you."

Then, with quick, heavy strides, he left the room.

I was left alone. I could still feel the heaviness of his hand and the coldness of his eyes. I felt a void in my stomach. Like someone who had not eaten for days, I was hungry and, at the same time, on the verge of throwing up. I did not want to cry. I was whirling in an endless vacuum. A few times, I tried to stand up to go to my bedroom, but I couldn't. None of my organs were under my control. I tried to light a cigarette or even release my knees from the grip of my hands, but I was unable to do so. I was like a helpless embryo folded in a fetal position. I was spinning around, and around, and around....

Time had stopped. There was no dimension to space. Sounds were dead and there was no movement in the air. I heard the front door open. The sound brought me back. My knees were frozen and there was a shooting pain in my back. I released my knees painfully and leaned back on the sofa. Then I asked Fatemeh Khanum, who was coming toward me, to help me stand up.

.18.

After a chaotic week, I decided to make an appointment to see Soraya. I had not been able to sleep most nights, and whenever I did doze, it was never for more than an hour. My chest ached all the time and I was constantly shivering. If I wanted to, I could seek the help of tranquilizers. Although Nargess had thrown the remainder of my reserves in the garbage, I could easily get them from a nearby chemist who let me have them without a prescription. But I was not prepared for the return of those horrifying nightmares. I hoped Soraya would have a cure other than pills.

Soraya was preparing to leave Iran. She was waiting for summer vacation so that she could take her son, too. Perhaps, by resorting to this deadline, Soraya was giving Abdol another chance to come to his senses and accompany them. But as soon as he had realized that Soraya was serious about her decision to leave Iran, Abdol gradually had alienated himself from her and dedicated his time and energy to the *Tudeh* Party.

The *Tudeh* Party was then openly advocating its collaboration with the government and the Mullahs. Many people believed that the party had adopted this policy to be able to penetrate the governmental departments and factories in preparation to seize power when the time was right. Whatever the policy was for, no one doubted that the *Tudeh* was prepared to do anything to gain the confidence of the Mullahs. They were actively involved in kicking leftist and Mojahedin members out of the offices and the factories by all kinds of tricks and conspiracies. The government welcomed this. It could get rid of the opposition without directly confronting its activists, whom people still liked and considered trustworthy.

The day I met with Soraya, she told me that Abdol had moved out of their home the day before. He had gone to live with his father, in that humble house where Colonel Nuri moved around in his wheelchair and delivered his fiery speeches to Hajji Jalali, who still came to see him twice a week. Abdol had asked Soraya to finalize their divorce before leaving the country. Despite all this, Soraya was happy that he had agreed to give their son, Sahand, to her.

She listened to what I told her very carefully. I told her everything. Knowing most of it already, she shook her head and began to talk.

"Luba... There is nothing you can do for Bardia. No one else can do anything for him, either. You'd best be concerned about yourself and Bahram."

I felt hopeless and overpowered.

"But I can't. I cannot leave him alone. My hope is that he may change. A year has not yet passed since his father's death and he has turned into someone whom I do not know at all. This is not natural. He has to change."

"He won't, Luba, he won't. Why do you think I'm taking my son out of this country? I don't want my son to be transformed into another Bardia. Just look around you. There are thousands of young boys like Bardia all over the place. Wherever you go, you see them with their machine guns on their shoulders. They are the guardians of a state which has given them all of their rights. What on earth could you or I give them instead so that they would abandon their masters and come and follow our ideas? Is there a child who voluntarily wants to be controlled by his parents?"

"Do you think these people can remain in power forever?"

She shook her head in despair.

"I don't think so. But that moment will not come so soon. Your problem is that once Bahram reaches the same age that Bardia is now, do you think that he wouldn't follow in his big brother's footsteps?"

It was the first time I realized the potential problem. Bahram's future, the future of an innocent little child who was being absorbed involuntarily into a dangerous world that could consume him as it had Bardia. But was it right to abandon Bardia for Bahram's sake?

"So I have to sacrifice one of the them for the other," I said.

Soraya was impatient.

"You don't sacrifice anyone. Your presence or absence has no effect on Bardia's life anymore. Hasn't he told you that already? You have to save Bahram. And then… well, your absence could have some effect on Bardia. Someday he may want to come back to you."

As Soraya continued to count the benefits that my departure from Iran could have for both of my children, I thought about Bardia. It seemed so impossible for me to leave him in Iran. He was not just an ordinary child to me. He was the only reminder I had of my native country. I viewed him as the last line connecting me to my past. To abandon him was to abandon a major part of myself; to abandon all of the memories I had carried out of my country in the form of a child named Bardia.

"This is not a simple thing. I have to think about it. I cannot decide so easily," I told Soraya.

• • • • •

Hajji and his friends' endeavors successfully released Ahmad from prison after three months. It was the end of April and spring was ripe. It was as pleasant and dreamlike as the previous springs, aside from the gloom of the people in Tehran. The weather was bright, with tiny clouds drifting over town from the summit of the Alborz Mountains, where Iranians believed to be the resting place of the mythological bird Simorgh, the guardian of Persia. The narrow alleys were filled with the fragrance of white jasmine trees, whose branches shed their essence into the scented, scattering breeze one can find only in Tehran.

Nargess welcomed Ahmad at the back door of the Ghasr prison. Once they were in the car, she said the words Ahmad had been so anxious to hear before going to jail.

"Will you marry me?" Nargess asked.

Instead of answering, Ahmad said, "I have painted a large portrait of Khomeini in jail."

Nargess repeated her question and Ahmad nodded. Nargess directly took him to a notary office that had already been informed about their marriage. Before they began the religious ceremony, Nargess told the men in the office, "You can do the rest once we're gone."

They signed the books and obtained the document proving they were husband and wife. Then they came straight home.

I needed to see Ahmad as soon as possible. I wanted to tell him that he should differentiate between Bardia and me, although I still knew that Bardia was an inseparable part of me.

As I was entering their apartment, Nargess told me that she had already explained everything to Ahmad and that I need not say anything about the past. I sat in front of him in an apartment that looked nothing like it did before. I looked at Ahmad's sinking eyes and felt that even if I wanted to say anything I would not be able to say it.

A blanket of oblivion enveloped the apartment. The bookshelves were empty. On the last shelf, a statue of a gray sable looked small and helpless in its loneliness. The naked walls were darkened in the areas that were once hidden behind picture frames. Ahmad sat on the edge of a blue sofa, as if he was prepared to stand up and leave at any moment. Behind him, there was no blue horizon of the sea, no golden bird, no red boat.

Clearly with tremendous effort, Nargess talked ceaselessly. Ahmad shifted his eyes between us without uttering a word. It was only when Nargess or I asked him a question that a tremble appeared on his right cheek and he responded by nodding or with one-word answers.

Later in the afternoon, Nargess came to my apartment.

"After you left, Ahmad went to bed and immediately fell asleep. His sleep is so deep that I think he has not been sleeping for days," she said. Then, worried and sorrowful, she added, "I don't know what they have done to him. He doesn't talk or answer my questions."

"Give him a chance. He'll be all right in a few days," I said.

Not only did he not regain his previously normal life, but, worse, he gradually drifted away into his silence and seclusion. I never came to know what they had done to him. Perhaps no one else found out, either. Whatever they had done to cause such a painful aloofness, they had done successfully.

Two weeks after his release from jail, Ahmad evacuated his apartment because, he said, he had no job and could not afford to pay the rent. As far as his job was concerned, he was right. Although he was not allowed to return to his job at the university, in the front hall of his college, his supervisors had hung a large painting of

Khomeini that bore Ahmad's signature. Khomeini glared at passers-by with threatening eyes under his bushy eyebrows. As for the rent, I insisted that Ahmad need not pay me. He did not accept my offer. He did not want Nargess to pay the rent, either. Instead, he rented a small nearby house that had three rooms and a small yard. He enclosed half of the yard in a greenhouse and began a small gardening business at home.

As Ahmad gradually sank deeper and deeper into his seclusion, Nargess became more restless. She left home early in the morning for her job at the City Council for a few hours and she returned home late at night. For sure, only Saeed knew where she was during those long hours when she was supposed to be at home. She would go to a makeshift home, which was often relocated due to security reasons, where she would prepare the artwork for the newspaper, which had been published in secret during the last few months. Now she was involved in writing for the paper, as well. Her articles, published under different pseudonyms, were intriguing, but directly against government policies.

After her ordeal with the committee, Nargess, too, had lost her carefree, happy mood, which had been replaced by a kind of hardened silence. Now those two parallel lines on both sides of her mouth were more visible than ever, making her seem older than her twenty-nine years. She hardly found time to see me. Others did not see her either. Whenever we called her, she said that she was very busy with her university dissertation, which was left unfinished at the advent of the revolution.

One Friday I saw her at Hajji's house.

"You are closing all the doors to yourself, just like me," I said.

She kissed me on the cheek.

"Don't you worry. I am not closing any doors. We have learned how to bow down today and straighten up the next day. This is a part of our daily lives. Our lives are like the history of our country — full of ups and downs, like the waves in the sea. We have no other choice but to restart again and again," she murmured in my ear. Then I told her I needed to talk to her.

"Anytime you want. Anytime," she said.

But it took me a long time to prepare myself for that meeting.

• • • • •

It was a morning in mid-June when I went to see Nargess in her small home. Ahmad was in his greenhouse, busy with his flowers. He seemed healthier than the last time I had seen him. But although he had gained some weight, his eyes were still dull and full of sorrow. Seeing me, he stopped working and came toward me, smiling. He said hello and asked if I was all right. Then, as if he had been called by someone else, he looked at his flowers, apologized, and returned to his work.

When Nargess led me inside the house, she said, "He doesn't talk to anyone."

"It'll be all right. He needs some time," I said.

Nargess led me to a small room furnished with what Nargess had brought from Hajji's house. I sat down on an orange sofa while Nargess went out to make some tea. I could see Ahmad working in the yard, like a well-trained gardener, placing a small flower into a pot. His careful movements reminded me of how carefully he used to put his paintings in their frames. I felt my heart sink as I remembered that I had my share in what had happened to him. I felt so guilty. If only I had not abandoned Bardia after Amin's death, if only I had left Iran with my children after he died....

Ahmad stood up and took the flowerpot into the greenhouse. When Nargess returned she told me that Ahmad now had a steady income from selling his flowers. Every Thursday at eight in the morning, a van would come to pick up the flowers for sale. Nargess said that Ahmad did not want to return to painting anymore. Whenever Nargess had asked him to try painting again, Ahmad had wept so pitifully that Nargess became worried and apologized profusely. Nevertheless, she was not prepared to give up.

"I have decided to leave Iran with Bahram," I said.

Even as I told her, I felt so sad about leaving Bardia behind. Nevertheless, a few weeks after my meeting with Soraya, and a few days after she left Iran with her own son, I had finally come to the conclusion that I had no other alternative but to leave the country and to leave Bardia, if I was serious about saving Bahram.

During those weeks, Bardia increasingly had become more rude and aggressive. I did not see much of him anymore. He came home very late at night and left early in the mornings. He did not bother to tell me anything about what he was doing. Sometimes accompanied by other guards, he brought home his weapons with him. Our relationship was very cold. Whenever I tried to approach him I faced a thick wall of indifference. I tried my best not to leave Bahram alone with him, but Bardia did not pay any attention to my presence. He told Bahram exciting stories in which he was the hero: he would invade the houses of anti-revolutionaries, arrest dangerous people, chase terrorists in cars. Bahram was fascinated and listened to him with rapt attention. Sometimes he became so excited that he clapped his hands together or jumped into Bardia's arms. And Bardia was as warm to him as he was cold to me. As soon as he arrived home, he took Bahram in his arms and to his room. He bought him several toys with the huge sums of money he made me give him. The toys were mostly replicas of guns and other sorts of weaponry. Sometimes he took the bullets out of his own gun and gave the naked weapon to Bahram while explaining how it worked.

Once, when he arrived home and found out that I had taken Bahram to a birthday party for one of his friends, Bardia got angry and shouted at me.

"Let it be the last time you send him anywhere without my permission!"

I had endured moments like this, yet I still had difficulty deciding whether or not to leave Iran. One day, I called Nargess at eight o'clock in the morning, when Bardia left for the day, and told her that I needed to talk about my plan with her.

The night before, I had not slept at all. At five o'clock in the morning, Bardia woke up to say his morning prayers. He usually did his homework after his prayers and before leaving home for school. It was only during these two hours that he attended to his lessons.

Usually he said his prayers in a loud voice that woke me up. He purposefully made a lot of noise to disturb my sleep. He noisily took showers and uttered his prayers as loudly as he could. I would duck my head under the quilt and try to go back to sleep. But that morning,

I had gotten out of bed and into the living room, where he liked to say his prayers.

On that bright, early morning, his figure seemed larger than ever. Although he soon was to turn fifteen, he looked like a young man of at least seventeen. I went into the kitchen, made a cup of coffee, and gazed at him. He stood in a courteous gesture toward the southeast, in the direction of the holy city of Mecca in Saudi Arabia. He had a picture of Khomeini in front of him. He bowed down and stood up with precision while incomprehensible Arabic words poured out of his mouth. I so wished that he would sit in front of me with his innocent smile and talk to me in the same way he talked a year ago. I wished that he would put his arms around my neck like he used to.

Bardia came into the kitchen. On finding me there, his eyes were filled with a surprise that took away his bitterness and stubbornness for a moment. He murmured, "Hi" and went toward the refrigerator.

"Have you woken up to say your prayers?" he asked.

There was a hint of teasing in his voice. His profile, lit by the refrigerator light, returned to that of a stern guard. I tried to ignore his question.

"Would you like me make you some breakfast?" I asked.

He took a bottle of milk from the refrigerator, poured some in a glass and said, "No."

Then he went out of the kitchen and back to his room.

Nargess smiled as if she had waited a long time for what I was telling her.

"I think you've made the right decision."

I explained to her how difficult it was for me to make that decision. I told her about what was going on at home and I knew that she did not need any convincing. She could easily imagine for herself. Others could understand, as well. I learned that there were many who watched what they said at Hajji's place on Fridays, while Bardia was present.

For some time, Bardia only came to his grandfather's house for Friday lunches. Esmat Khanum still praised him lavishly with her flattering words; in return, Bardia was very warm toward her. He kissed her and Hajji on the cheeks. While smiling indifferently at others, he sat at the table, had his lunch, and hastily left the house. During the short time that he was there, the atmosphere of the room became unbearably heavy. Gradually the number of people who attended Hajji's Friday lunches began to dwindle. While she was still in Tehran, Soraya brought her son only when she knew that Bardia had left. Abdol's sister, Homeira, and her children did not show up at all. Others had their own excuses for not attending Hajji's lunches. Finally, the only people left at the table were my family, Nargess, Saeed's parents, and Abdol. Still, everybody kept silent in Bardia's presence. Usually Hajji and Saeed's father talked about trivial issues and others pretended to listen. Only Abdol, who sometimes sat next to Bardia, would ask him about various daily issues. He listened to Bardia as attentively as one would listen to an old, experienced man.

"I've decided to go now. But I can't tell Bardia about this. He won't let me take Bahram with me," I said.

What I really wanted to know was whether Hajji could get Bardia's consent. Bardia still respected his grandfather. Sometimes I felt that he somehow dreaded Hajji. Hajji was still respected by Bardia's superiors. Bardia knew that most of the committee leaders came to see Hajji, the ministers and the public prosecutor held great esteem for him, and the President talked to him on the telephone. Whenever people wanted to introduce Bardia to others, they would mention that he was the grandson of Hajji Jalali. It was usually after Hajji's name that they would add, "And the son of martyred Dr. Jalali."

Thus, he had to respect Hajji, too. Perhaps Hajji himself, by ignoring what Bardia did, and refraining from putting pressure on him, had done his own part in keeping Bardia's respect. What I wondered was if Hajji would interfere and persuade Bardia to allow me leave Iran with Bahram.

I was almost sure that Hajji would accept my request even if Bardia tried to cause complications. Hajji, though deeply conservative, had his own beliefs and would not stray from them. After Amin's death, he told me that he considered me the guardian of my children and would help me if I ever wanted to leave Iran. I was sure that he would not change his mind.

I knew that Nargess was not going to answer my question without carefully examining all of the considerations involved. This characteristic made her quite different from most of the Iranian women I had met in my life. She was silent when I finished talking. I knew that her cunning mind was searching for the wisest course of action. Then, while playing with her hair with her small and delicate fingers, she answered me.

"I think you should go without letting Bardia know. Actually, no one should know that you're leaving until you reach England. It's useless to try to get Bardia's consent. He may accept it outwardly but he'll try a lot of different tricks to prevent you from taking Bahram."

"Even if your father was involved?" I asked.

As if ready for this question, Nargess answered me right away.

"I'll talk to him. He could get your passport renewed without anyone knowing. They don't issue passports that easily nowadays. But I don't think it would be wise to say a word to Bardia."

I could not hide my anxiety.

"But Bardia will be furious."

When she gazed at me, it was evident that she could read my fear in my eyes.

"He'll get mad, in any case. But the important thing is for you to be able to leave here…."

She kept talking and I could see how much more experienced she was than me. I felt humbled in her presence; I wondered how, in a backward society and a religious family, she had been mentally able to grow so much.

Once she was finished discussing Bardia's probable reaction and what I had to do until the time came to leave Iran, she suddenly changed the subject.

"Don't you want to see Saeed before you leave the country?"

Four months had passed since the night I had talked to Saeed in private — the night before Nargess and Ahmad were arrested by the guards. I had seen him a few times at Hajji's house and, without having the courage to look into his eyes, had exchanged a few words with him. Even if I wanted to say more, it was impossible in the presence of the others. He, too, had gradually distanced himself from me. Before the arrests, he would sit next to me and chat with me like other members of the family. But during the last few weeks, he had not even telephoned me. Yet, I still loved him and missed him in my life.

"No. I don't want to see him. I'll write him a letter when I get to England."

Nargess smiled. "Even once?"

"No. I don't feel comfortable facing him. I dread myself."

"You think you might change your mind about leaving here?"

"No. I just don't want to promise him anything that I might not be able to deliver in an unknown future."

Nargess raised her head and looked out at Ahmad, whose profile could be seen amongst the leaves of an acacia tree. Sun rays passed through the lace curtains and lit Nargess's face. She was like a statue standing under the diffused light of a museum — the statue of an unknown goddess so beautiful that one could not take one's eyes away from it.

"I do not know what will happen in the days to come," I continued. "I don't even know if Saeed will ever leave this country. I don't know what is waiting for me once I get out. It is not right to promise anything so far into an uncertain future."

The statue's face began to liven up. There was a deep and pleasant smile on her lips.

"I don't blame you. I admire the way you think. This is exactly what differentiates the women in this part of the world from you. We usually get involved in situations as a result of moments of extreme emotion and undertake things that are beyond our means. Then we pay for it in a painful, even hateful, way for the rest of our lives. Yet we're proud that we have remained faithful to our promises. We actually label our lies as our faithfulness."

I was dauntless in my next question.

"Haven't you married Ahmad in just the same way?"

She hastily shook her head.

"No. I had not promised him anything. I had not promised to become his wife before he went to jail. After that it was I who decided. I wanted to marry him. And I still want to remain his wife. Soraya believes that I have done so because I felt guilty. Because my nephew has done this to him. She may be right. But still, as long as I love him and enjoy being with him the way I do now, I have not lied to him or to myself."

Then, she moved her hand in the air as if trying to push something away.

"Let's forget these things now…. When do you want to leave?" she asked.

"Now that I've made up my mind, the sooner the better."

●　●　●　●　●

Upon hearing my decision, Hajji was neither surprised nor resentful. Tears appeared in his eyes and he said, "This is better. At least that innocent boy will do better than his brother."

Unlike Saeed and Nargess, who believed that things could soon change, Hajji believed it was impossible to unseat the Mullahs. He had come to that conclusion soon after Bani-Sadr had become the first President of the Republic. Bani-Sadr was a moderate politician elected mostly by the supporters of the National Front and the middle to upper classes. Hajji, like others, had noticed that the new President was unable to challenge the Mullahs or to set up a centralized political power in the country. Nevertheless, Hajji had not given up. He still planned to weaken the Mullahs and the extremists in the government by helping Bani-Sadr and his team with his financial and moral support. He could not foresee that within only one year he was to be targeted by the wrath of the extremist fraction and forced to be housebound until the end of his life.

From the moment Nargess had informed Hajji about my decision, he had begun his efforts to get new passports for Bahram and me. Yet, it was a month and a half before I had my passport in my hands. Each day seemed like an endless month to me.

Bardia, now fifteen, had become tougher than ever. I had stopped showing any reaction to what he did or said. I tried to enjoy the short time I had with him as much as possible. But I could not find joy in any moment of that period. I looked at him as if he had gone mad. Everyday I asked myself if it was right to leave. And every time, Bahram's presence and my thoughts about his future confirmed my decision to go.

When I got my passport, I could not resist my tremendous desire to see Saeed. I told Nargess that I wanted to see him. She nodded in despair and said, "He left Tehran only last night for Turkmenistan. He won't be back until the end of the week."

He did not return from that trip until my last day in Iran. It took me nine more years to see him again, this time thin and broken, with a tuft of white hair on his temple, and clutching a piece of paper in his hand that declared his status as a refugee. He came toward me, from the throng of passengers arriving in Heathrow Airport from Turkey, and held me in his arms, as tightly as he had held me on that autumn night at Golsara.

.19.

On August 7, 1980, three days before the anniversary of Amin's death, I took Bahram with me to Hajji's house with the excuse of helping Esmat Khanum for the ceremonies. I had told Bardia he should visit Hajji's for the next two nights. He had nodded without knowing that he would see Bahram and me only one more night. We were to fly out of Iran at eleven o'clock the next morning.

I took just a small bag that contained our passports, two sweaters, a few other trivial things, and Marta's tape. I hid the bag under the bed in Nargess's room at Hajji's house. By not bringing a suitcase, I would avoid the control check at the airport customs. Hajji was to come to the airport with us and see that everything went smoothly. In those days, people often were told that they were not allowed to leave the country only after they arrived at the airport. Some people were even arrested there. Hajji did not want Nargess to come to the airport. He had told her, "Remember, if Bardia or anyone else ever asks you about this, your answer should be that you were not aware about their decision. It was something between Luba and Hajji."

Nargess was clearly worried. I had seldom seen her in that mood. As soon as Esmat Khanum left the room, Nargess held me in her arms and kissed me. Esmat Khanum was very busy. She sometimes murmured to herself, sometimes wept for a while, and, at the same time, supervised Sedigheh Khanum, who was preparing everything for the ceremony which was to be held three days later. I could picture her on that day, weeping and beating her chest, calling Bahram's name along with Amin's and maybe even mine.

According to Esmat Khanum's orders, Sedigheh Khanum brought a large portrait of Amin into the living room and put it on a chair right in front of me. Amin was wearing a striped blue tie and a deep blue suit. He was smiling. I looked at him for a long time and felt that I did not hate him anymore. He was an unfamiliar figure that belonged to a faraway and forgotten past; a past of which I had only a faint picture in my mind. I told Nargess how I felt. She turned and stood in front of me. Her slim and beautiful figure seemed livelier than ever. She smiled and said, "Only love can wipe out hate." Her face was radiating. She had again turned into the statuette of an unknown goddess. I could not help watching her. She had always been a symbol of love and gentleness to me, an Anahita who comes to bring love and kindness to our world. Nowadays, I sometimes think about how difficult it should have been for her to live in a time and place, darkened and contaminated by sheer hatred.

That night, when Bardia arrived, I went to him and took him in my arms. He waited for a while in my arms and then moved away. He kissed Esmat Khanum, who had just entered the room and was praising him as usual. Then he moved toward Amin's picture, stood in front of it for a while, and, with his head bowed down, sat on a chair next to the picture. Bahram went to him and embraced his legs. Like a sleepwalker, I, too, went toward him, sat on the floor next to his legs, leaned my head on his knee, and burst into tears. I could hear my loud voice filling the room like a thunder. I do not know how long I was in that position, but I remember hearing Nargess talking to me. "You and Mom have been crying for so long. At least have some consideration for Bahram."

Bardia stood up, gently took Bahram out of my arms and said, "Let's go to the other room and watch television with Grandpa."

When I looked up, he was leaving the room. Our eyes locked for a moment. His face was covered with a deep sorrow, like the year before, when he was told about Amin's death. His eyes looked like mine once again. And I still loved them.

Those eyes followed me until the plane took off and began to fly over Tehran, which was covered with a blanket of dust. I looked away from the ground and from the brick and cement buildings, which, from that height, looked like skeletons rising from their graves. I gazed at the sky. It was the same turquoise sky by which Iran is known all over the world. And the sun was the same sun to whose glory the Iranians used to swear before the invasion of Arab Muslims.

.20.

But that was not the last time I saw Bardia. I saw him again ten years later, a year ago, when he came to London as the economic representative of the Islamic Republic. I saw him when he came out of the embassy to get into a diplomatic car that was waiting for him. Bahram and I had waited for hours outside the embassy just to catch a glimpse of him. We were standing amid a large crowd that had gathered to protest against the repressive policies of the Iranian government. I tightly held both Bahram's arm and the metal fence set up by the police, as I tried not to let the force of the crowd move me.

Walking tall, with a short mustache and a thick beard, Bardia appeared between embassy bodyguards and British policemen. He was limping but seemed proud and in full control. He had no resemblance to my Bardia. He went toward the embassy's car. An egg flew from the crowd and landed on his head. A narrow yellow line ran down his forehead. He stopped, took a handkerchief out of his pocket, and cleaned his forehead with an anxiousness similar to that of his childhood. Then he looked at the crowd. He was my Bardia, his eyes were just like mine, filled with bewilderment and empty of any anger.

I wished I could jump out of the crowd, hold him in my arms and shout, "My son... My son...."

A young girl in her teens, standing next to me, began to yell.

"You're a murderer.... You're all murderers!"

Bardia disappeared in the darkness of the car. I looked at the girl. Her beautiful black eyes were full of tears and her cheeks were trembling. I could see that it was Nargess. I tried to hold her in my arms. Bahram took my hand and murmured, "Mother, it's better if we go."

GLOSSARY

Bazaar: The large market which was a traditional power center.

Confederation of Iranian Students: A loose organization of many of the opponents of the Shah outside of Iran.

Great Satan: The Islamic Republic's term for the United States.

Mojahedin: An Islamic-Marxist political group which were very active at the start of the revolution. They became the major opponents of the Islamic Republic.

National Front Party: The inheritors of Prime Minister Mohammad Mossadegh's liberal party which had ruled Iran from 1951 to 1953. Their most notable achievement was the nationalization of oil.

Samovar: An urn used to boil water to brew tea. A samovar is often on to supply tea in an Iranian's house or office.

SAVAK: The acronym for the state secret police during the Shah's reign.

Sherbet: Cold sweet syrupy fruit drink.

Tudeh Party: The Soviet-supported Iranian communist party.

Translator's Afterword

Shokooh Mirzadegi is one of the finest contemporary Iranian writers the Islamic Republic has successfully managed to force into exile.

Although some of Mirzadegi's short stories and plays have already appeared in English and French, this is her first novel translated into English. Nevertheless, this single book is enough to show the extent of the losses suffered by the literary milieu inside Iran due to the mass exodus of Iranian literary figures after the advent of the 1979 revolution. The only consoling fact is that such books, despite being banned by the Islamic regime, have been smuggled into Iran and heavily copied and read, especially by young readers.

Shokooh Mirzadegi was born in 1944. She was married at the age of sixteen and soon became the mother of two daughters. Later, she studied child psychology at Tehran Teachers University.

I remember her first visit to the office of the Iranian literary magazine, *Ferdowsi*, on an evening in 1967 in Tehran, escorted by her then-husband, who introduced her as a potential writer. He wanted her to use her married name, Farhang. She soon became a staff writer for our magazine and began to publish short stories and poems. She also published in other Persian magazines and newspapers. Her first collection of short stories, *Bíqarárí-há-ye Páyedár* (Permanent Restlessness), was published in book form in 1972.

A year later, I, along with many of our friends, were shocked to read in the Iranian evening newspapers that she had been arrested, along with several other Iranian writers, musicians, and filmmakers, charged with conspiring against the monarchy. The government prosecutor asked for her execution by firing squad. She was imprisoned for two years and her saga ended only when she and other imprisoned writers agreed to appear on Iranian television and apologize for their deeds. Two of the detained — a poet and a writer — who refused to do so, were executed.

Once out of prison, Mirzadegi divorced her husband and began a period of rehabilitation. It took her more than two years to recover from her bitter experience and to begin publishing again, this time under her own surname. The very self-explanatory title of her new collection of short stories was *Ágház-e Dovvom* (The Second Beginning). During the next two years, she wrote two plays—*Man Harkat Míkonam, Pas Hastam* (I Run, Therefore I Am) and *Ta'bídí-ye Sál-e 3000* (Prisoner of the Year 3000), whose staging was banned; published three storybooks for children; and wrote a travel account of her trip to Mecca entitled *Sá'y-e Hajar* (The Struggles of Hagar). While the former titles clearly show their political connotations, the latter is the beginning of her serious involvement in the women's rights movement and her writings as a feminist.

She was permitted to leave for the West at the end of 1977. She returned to Iran a year later, just before the ousting of the monarchy. After the revolution she was arrested by the Islamic government, charged with collaborating with the Shah's regime. Fortunately, her plight was publicized and through pressure from the United Nations Commission for Human Rights, she was released after a month.

She immediately began her journalistic activities and her daily column in the newspaper *Bámdád* became very popular. This did not last long. The newspaper and her column were banned and she fled for England, where her two daughters were attending school.

Once settled in London, she embarked on the publication of *Mamnú'e-há* (Forbidden Works)—a literary magazine sponsored by the famous Iranian humorist, Manouchehr Mahjoubi. Its title revealed its contents. A year later, she published one of the first post-revolutionary political magazines outside Iran called *Moqávemat* (Resistance). It was in this magazine that she invited me to join her as a writer. Thus, our friendship resumed in London.

In 1984, she decided to dedicate her time to her literary and social writings and separate herself from direct political involvement. She was one of the first Iranian writers who joined me and a few others to establish the Society of Iranian Writers and Artists in Britain. She also founded the Iranian Women's organization in the England during that period. Then, in 1989, Shokooh and I decided to publish a cultural periodical called *Púyeshgarán* (The Dynamists). The aim was to promote the modern Persian literary and artistic trend which was taking shape outside Iran, despite the wishes of the Islamic regime.

She began to publish her new short stories in *Púyeshgarán*. They were immediately recognized for their imagination and literary craftsmanship. At the same time she worked on her first novel, the English translation of which is now in front of you.

We were married in January, 1990 in London. She finished her novel three years later and called it *Bígáneh-yí dar Man* (That Stranger Within Me). It was an immediate success. The first print sold out within five months. It won two literary prizes: "Sepás" in London and "Bárán" in Stockholm. The judges for both prizes were from amongst the best literary critics and writers outside Iran. They declared the book "The Best Persian Novel of 1993." The work went through a second printing in 1994 and, again, sold out in eight months. It went to a third printing in May of 1996.

I was the first reader of the book, which Shokooh has kindly dedicated to me. Once I finished the book, I was very impressed with its richness and intriguing structure. Seeing its potential appeal to a wider international readership, I decided to translate it into English. This coincided with our move from London. In May 1994, we immigrated to the United States and settled in Denver, Colorado.

Although I have almost finished the chronology of the author's life, there is still one point that I feel obliged to disclose to the reader. Presently the English title of the book is *That Stranger Within Me*. I am not happy with the word "stranger," that stands for the word *bígáneh* in the original Persian title of the book. My original translation of the title was *That Alien in Me*. But, the editors and the publisher of the book rightly found my version more suitable for a science-fiction book rather than a fictional and realistically narrated story of a foreign woman caught in the web of the Islamic revolution in Iran.

To me, it is an unfortunate fact that the usage of the word "alien" has become associated with science-fiction creatures. People even tend to forget that holders of green cards in the United States are known as Alien Residents. In fact, anyone coming from another culture could be called an alien by the citizens of the host society. We should not forget that, etymologically speaking, "lien" means all your belongings, mostly in the shape of landed properties, which connect you to a certain geographical location. An alien is someone who loses this connection. Thus, immigrants and foreigners are not strangers. They are aliens coming not from outer space but from lands far apart and far different from here and now.

Although Shokooh Mirzadegi never tells us who this alien is in her novel, we definitely come to recognize that her alien could not be a stranger who lives in the conscious or subconscious mind of the novel's narrator. In fact, this dilemma between ambiguity and clarity is the celebrated outcome of an implicit style used for narrating a very complicated plot with several interesting and, at times, unforgettable characters. It is the result of a deliberate and masterfully produced mixture of a series of subjective and objective observations, revealing a chaotic, ancient and fragile world on the brink of a fundamental revolution which is designed to take it back in history and time. The ensuing events are to change drastically the destiny of the novel's narrator, as well as that of all contemporary Iranians.

To me, this book is about alienation in that variegated and multidimensional meaning of the word and I still would like to call it *An Alien in Me*.

By now, the reader should have guessed that I love this book and its writer.

More than a few individuals have helped with this translation. The publisher and I would like to express our gratitude to Maryam Enayat, Susanne Knopp, Alex Robbins, Mamad Shirazi, Parvaneh Shirzad and Shahriar Zanganeh who read and commented on the translation. Naturally, they are not responsible for any errors.

—   Esmail Nooriala,
Denver, October 1996